SHADOW LIGHTS

SHADOW LIGHTS

AND THE THREE BRAVE KNIGHTS

MARGA RITA

XULON PRESS

Xulon Press
2301 Lucien Way #415
Maitland, FL 32751
407.339.4217
www.xulonpress.com

Edited by Xulon Press.

Printed in the United States of America.

ISBN-13: 978-1-54562-084-7

Contents

ACKNOWLEDGEMENTS

All praises and thanksgiving to *Jesus*, my Saviour, the source of my wisdom and strength.

Thanks and love to my husband, Archie, for the support.

Thanks and love to my beautiful children, Andrew, Matthew, Angelo, Meg, and Ava. You are my inspiration.

"Now to him who is able to do immeasurably more than all we ask or imagine, according to his power that is at work within us." Ephesians 3:20

Chapter 1:
The Forbidden Crossing

Argos plummeted. The smell of death lingered in the air. Suddenly, the diamond ring in his right index finger turned into ruby—his *memory stone*, the storage of his memories. Remembering the night of the massacre, his nostrils flared. Before him, the glittery sky gloomed.

Rainbow lights scarred the dark sky, stirred up by the blaring trumpet. His terrified eyes turned vigilant. His weakened, freshly oiled, stork-like wings gained strength. While in midair, he unleashed his flaming sword; its gilded hilt bearing wing engraves. He landed on both feet. Dust flew. His leafy ears wiggled, deafened by the eerie silence greeting him—the nests emptied. Suddenly, the towering, luscious canopies shook. His name echoed in the air, spoken by many voices. He clenched his broad jaws, bracing for a melee. The voices turned up. A bright light flashed overhead. He spun on the balls of his feet, ready to draw blood, but the rainbow lights volleying down the plateau transformed into badly-wounded *Luceres* at touchdown. Their memory stones of varied gemstones blinked faintly.

Clanking metals boomed in the sky. More colorful lights fell off their orbits. He narrowed his eyes while his wings marshaled. About to join the fray, a rattling noise rang out. He froze, shocked by its forbidden presence. The dense bushes behind his fallen fellows shook hard. He raced against it at once, flashing in a speed of light. His blazing sword went ahead of him, burning like a torch. Its hungry snarling and rumbling belly slithering over the flattened grasses blasted his ears. The wind blew his way. He halted. A terrible stench filled the air.

Fountains of blood spurted over the plateau. Death rattles roared. Bloody faces flashed in his mind, the last, a snarling monstrous, ebony vermin with fierce yellowish eyes and large white fangs dripping with blood about to swallow him. He tipped backward with his flaming sword stretched out. Its yellow blaze burned across his face. He watched his name etched on his sword's blade float amidst the blaze, spoken repeatedly by his bereaved mother, her fresh farewell haunting him.

"Argos. Argos. Come back!"

He gasped, startled to see himself striking the dreary sun. His haunted mind cleared up. The streaks of blood in his memory stone faded. He dropped his sword. Its blaze faded. He let out a sigh of relief, while his wings shed dust.

"I still have time. The pest is still asleep," he mumbled.

The grinding noise behind him came to a full stop. He cranked his neck around. Slightly mildewed vines crawled over the mouth of the cave, hiding the City of Refuge in plain sight. The cries of desperation of his fellows echoed in his mind. Keeping a stiff upper lip, he launched away. His wings stayed straddled out of habit. His pulse quickened seeing the sulfuric blaze filtering through the chinks of towering, fragile white oaks faint. The rutted, cramped pathway darkened every step he took. His thick eyebrows twitched. Beads of sweat bubbled on his aquiline nose, an eyesore he described as worse than the adolescent acne he had weeks ago.

A shadow fell on him. The owl hooted. Herds of dark clouds marched in like soldiers wielding swords. The glittery sky bled. His shimmering shadow crawled away from his feet. Frantic, he fished out from his left pocket a golden chain holding a fist-sized vintage compact mirror riddled with tiny, cut diamonds on the rim with an engraved pair of wings and a monogram of his name.

"This is a cheat. We, weapons, are not supposed to use mirrors while in a battle. It holds off time. But desperate times call for desperate measures," he said, cracking it open.

His eyes faltered. Dark spots covered the mirror, forbidding him to see his reflection. The hordes of dark clouds multiplied. He turned toward the dehydrated hills he last saw looked like heaps of emeralds, hoping not to hear metallic noises—the *Deorcs,* former *Luceres* who broke ranks, the king's nocturnal army hunting them down.

The cold evening dew descended. His feathers fluttered. Flurries blew in. His eyes turned white. The day dissolved fast. The temperature dropped. He gritted his teeth, grasping the weird changes—the hated light revealed the truth, the cold, such was the heart of the king. Around him the fragile trees turned leprous, like candlesticks minus the fire. He pursed his glossed lips, grieving over those snuffed *candles of life* – life monitors of those who didn't make it to the sanctuaries.

He pressed on, struggling to keep his balance over the bleached, parched ground. A thick fog carrying dead leaves crept in. A pocket swirled him by. His face paled, as he picked up a disembodied gravelly man's voice—the king's! It came in a whisper, and in a blink, it drawled at his face and spoke; the voice surrounded him.

Out of the ground comes a sound that will bring light into plight!

The rattling noise that had drilled in his head returned. His flaming sword blazed. He hustled up eastward, determined to escape the king's dark spell, which brought the pest. Trampling the frosted ground he imagined was soaked with the blood of his fellows, his eyes narrowed.

"I will wake up *Justice*. But first, I need to find the *Truth*," he said through clenched teeth.

Diseased bushes clawed him. Plucked feathers flew. Smelling a whiff of the aromatic oil he used on his wings, he quickly twisted his body. He then clapped his wings like cymbals, dispersing his scent, making sure the *Deorcs* won't trace it back to the cave. Snow drifted. Uprooted, blighted shrubs rolled away, revealing floor scrapes, which he identified they had caused. He turned tail. His eyes quivered while searching for the translucent light to filter through the dark horizon: the morning sun in Evergreen.

The night fell with the force of an avalanche. His sword's blaze flickered. Running blind, he sniffed hard, like a dog on point, searching for any warm fragrance spurted by neon light posts – blinking, head-sized, rainbow neon flowers bursting with sweet, glimmering seeds—vanilla, honey, caramel, lily, citrus, and orange marmalade flavors. None hailed him. Lightning struck. Thunder roared. The constant flashes exposed the missing neon flowers sprawled on the ground. Stems thawed, heads crushed and bleeding colorful, he lost hope.

The ground shook. The leprous trees started decking in a domino. He scurried away with effort, struggling to keep his balance against the uneven, icy floor. From the corner of his eye, he saw the wreck-trail heading his way. The rattling noise he couldn't dispose off chased him – the trees being uprooted by the bitter cold. The ground shook harder, too hard, and he feared it would break open the abyss – the pest's nest. Suddenly, sleeping memory stones buried under the dirt were thrown at impact. The stones sparkled in a split second.

Light returned to the pitch dark sky. Dazzled, he covered his eyes. His present mind reminded him he was merely witnessing the last shared memory of the stones. Colors exploded. The memory stones took shape into *Luceres* wearing plain clothes, like sackcloths.

"Grassroots," he surmised.

The trumpet blared. Their wings whirred, but a drizzle prevented them working. His eyes were as large as saucers, seeing them bathed in blood. Shortly, they fell on their feet clutching their chests. The treetops shook. A shadow holding a silver cup perched on a tree. Furious over the revelation, he marched forward with his drawn sword, dying to silence his pestering hiccups. Instead of advancing though, he found himself withdrawing, pulled back to his reality.

"The cupbearer! Just an *article!* Of what courage!" he roared, striking the decking trees. "Face me, coward! Fight a *weapon!*" The wing stencil on his gilded breastplate glimmered.

Chopped, burning logs lined the dark woods. The flying embers crackled. More trees fell. He rushed away, striking all obstructing trees he wished were *Deorcs* – weapons and articles alike. What a heroic feat it would have been, he thought to himself, reducing the king's army in one blow. His adrenaline shot up. On his right, a surging dark shadow pounced on him.

He landed blocks away, in a face-plant. He grimaced, feeling his torn shoulder blades and skewed wings. On his right, a huge, felled tree confessed. The wind howled. The diseased, frosted bushes shook around him. He gripped his flaming sword, only to realize he lost it. Behind the flying debris, he saw its dying blaze. Suddenly, he couldn't breathe. Something cold and scaly was choking him. Shortly, he was flying again, but against his will. Collared to the tallest tree, he witnessed Shadow Light's demise. His heart sank. No moon. No stars. No glowing *Luceres* cruising the sky. Shadow Lights, the kingdom of *Truth, Love and Justice* – the *Fruits of Light,* the sacred land of the Nephelim, his ancestors, now desecrated by the cloak of lies.

"*Umbra!*" he cried.

The king's dark spell hummed eerily over the terrified hills.

"I-I won't serve you!" His voice cracked.

Flurries attacked. His gilded breastplate turned silvery. He grumbled, outraged by its color. He tried to wipe it, but the noose around his neck – as revealed by his corroding armor – strangled him tighter, ripping his head off his body. His bruised neck ruptured. The bitter cold pierced his flesh. Railroad of blisters broke out on his papery skin, which was now beginning to turn bluish. A hole formed in his chest. He tried to produce a healing light, but his numbed fingers wouldn't wiggle a bit. Cold to the bones, his thinning, skewed feathers stood up like nails, while his waist-long blond hair froze like a broomstick. Wasted, he dropped his head unwillingly. His conscience screamed against his act of surrender. Below, his name flickered, buried under the pent-up flood of dark mist. His plucked feathers glimmered in a puddle of blood.

A blur of white shadows perched. His heart jumped. His rescuers came! He waited for them to release him, but they maintained distance. Worse, they reeked. They bore the same awful scent he found airborne at his exit, the reason why he fell from his orbit. His jaded eyes faltered. They were deceased. Their dead memory stones spoke back to him. Shortly, his memory stone blinked, as if nudging. The cave appeared before him, his stone projecting its image.

"The City of Refuge!" he screamed.

He immediately stabbed the noose with his wingtips, aiming to create space. Twice. Thrice. He kept on trying. The noose remained tight. Wondering why his effort yielded no results, he looked over his shoulders with strain. He saw a glimpse of his broken wings. They were frozen. His torn shoulders dropped. His effort was only happening in his head. A shadow of guilt darkened his eyes. He cut short their annihilation. He could hear in his spirit the chaos and bitter cries occupying the city, brought upon by his flickering candle of life. Tears welled in his eyes. His mother's cry was the loudest and most painful.

"I killed her. Twice," he sobbed.

His memory stone's sparkle faded. He bid it goodbye while praying in his heart his stored memories would fall into the right hands. Yet, he doubted his prayers would be answered. No one would be willing to step out of the sanctuaries. His leap of faith weighed heavy on him, a death wish his heartbroken mother described otherwise.

He started drifting down to the seabed of the abyss. Inside its belly, his spirit contorted, bullied by the darkness lording over him, screaming hatred against his light. The king's spell drowned him. It blasted his eardrums, yet it played like a lullaby in his dying spirit. His constricted body started numbing, turning into a corpse. His failing heartbeat played like a broken metronome, beating in prolonged intervals and sluggish tempo. About to sleep, he saw with half an eye a glimpse of the translucent light waiving from the recesses of the dark forest. He groaned in disappointment, the noise sounding like a death rattle. His mission was within reach! Or at least nearer, he brooded, feeling a nip of its warm breath on his cold cheeks.

Goosebumps struck. A strong hand pulled him up, resurrecting him from the depths. He gasped, released from the cold darkness he felt held him up like a straight jacket. His leafy ears wiggled. His heart picked up a strong beat. He wiggled his numbed fingers. They finally obeyed! A gentle light clapped. He looked up and saw a fist-sized ball of light dancing across his face. For a moment he thought it was a plucked feather. Snorting, his nostrils flared. It smelled like the aroma of a watered land! Mossy! Of the earth!

"E-Evergreen!" he croaked.

Gravity pulled him down, as the frozen branch hoisting him up melted. He said goodbye to the suspended abyss and to his deceased fellows also, promising them vengeance. The moment his feet landed, he limped his way toward his sword. It glowed at his touch. The ball of light went ahead, flashing like a headlight. The diseased branches, covered with hoarfrost, melted as it made its way. The cramped pathway opened. His forehead creased; he was at a loss over its power. He dragged his skewed wings, following it faithfully through shortcuts he didn't know exist.

"Why does it know Shadow Lights better?" His wonder swelled.

The *Omniscient Gate* came into view – the skywalk between Shadow Lights and Evergreen. It glistened, calling for him. He scampered in haste. While climbing up the slippery steps of the bridge, the king's voice emerged from the haunted woods. He stumbled. The ball of light clapped over his head. He pressed on. Reaching the deck, which turned into an ice skating rink, bright lights sparkled inside the darkened tunnel. His pupils dilated.

"Either way, death awaits me," he said, feeling a chill crawling in his spine.

Thick flurries rained. The king's voice screamed at his face. He cupped his ears. The king's voice pinned him to the ground after, like a strong hand stopping him from stemming the tide. He fought back, but he heard the rattling noise again. It sounded way too close, like the pest's mouth was hovering over his head, about to swallow him whole. His grip on his sword weakened. His knees felt like jelly. Suddenly, the ball of light whizzed past him. Touched by its radiance, a different energy swept him. He stood up, burning with anger.

The ball of light exploded. The flurries died. The king's voice retreated. His jaws dropped and it stayed that way for a moment. "W-who are you?" he asked, realizing it was a *Lucere*.

The ball of light flew back to the tunnel. The grits of crystal stones embedded in the walls glowed and made long hazes of light beams–*witness stones* keeping an eye on wandering *Luceres*. Touched by the rays, it transformed into a vague image of a male *Lucere.* His purple coat made of silk sparkled in the dark.

"Prince Elijah?" Argos couldn't believe his eyes. He called him again, to no avail. "Stop! Give me the *Chronicles of Light!* We have to expose the king's sins!" His voice echoed.

Hiccups boomed. Furious, he spun and struck the air, eyeing the silver spark emerging from the treetops. The sound of dripping water drenched his sword's fury. A stream of blood – the poisonous wine – flowed out from the woods.

"I will fight you *mano y mano* on my return!" he promised, before plodding across the bridge.

A loud whizzing erupted in the air: Frozen crimson flint icicles hurtling the frigid air like shooting arrows, mobilized by the cupbearer hiding in the dark. He frantically entered the tunnel. The witness stones clapped at his face, like flashes of a camera capturing his entry. He squirmed, feeling embarrassed. Behind him, the towering, winged metal railings rang. Exiting, the tepid air greeted him. He found Prince Elijah standing in front of a wall of streaming lights. The ground below it was tarred, about three meters wide. The wing stencil on his gilded breastplate glimmered, touched by a ray of light.

"Don't cross the *Gray Border* again!" he implored.

Flint icicles entered the tunnel. He looked over and saw a handful bleeding and broken on the dusty floor, once macadamized. The Gray Border sizzled. He panned back and saw Prince Elijah crossing. His head grew big, feeling the hurtling icicles within a hair away. He galloped toward the Gray Border with his face stained with guilt. From the corner of his eye, he saw the red tips of the flint icicles about to impale him. He dove into the wall.

A furious storm greeted him. He glanced briefly over his shoulders. The wall of light stood behind him. Inside the tarred line, a chasm filled with raging dark waters roared below him. He flapped his broken wings, eager to reach the other end. His eyebrows furrowed, at a loss as to how the three-meter width stretched into a wide creek. The water licked his feet. His ears wiggled, hearing growling from underneath. He kept his head up. Dark sky hovered over his head. His eyes turned saucer-like when a surge of tidal wave rushed his way.

"Where is the sun?" he asked in desperation.

A faint light flickered ahead. He focused on it. It kept on swelling as he reached for it. When his fingertips touched it, white noise followed. Crossing over, he squirmed, zapped by the streaming lights falling on him like a fading waterfall. He flapped his broken wings to dry, feeling drenched and dirty. The midget trees rustled. The ringing in his ears stopped. He lunged with his sword, startled by the tickling, peeled grasses rolling back to cover the tarred ground. The trembling ground ceased. Tiny wild flowers bowed down before him as if welcoming his trespass. His heart fluttered nervously.

Water dripped. He checked his feet and saw a small puddle from the ice flakes in his frozen wings melting. The crispy, broken feathers started to relax. He spread his wings, letting the sunlight in. Bathing, his face was rapturous. He felt the sun's warm bite penetrating his cold flesh, making his blood boil, reaching his entire being, his face lastly. The chain holding his compact mirror jiggled. He smirked, wishing he could see the color on his face. His jaundice slowly disappeared. The blowing warm wind untangled his hair. Feasting at the bright sky, his azure eyes sparkled like sapphires. He opened his dry lips, wishing to express his gratitude, but the pale clouds pushed him back.

"Evergreen," he said, feeling iffy.

Suddenly, everything moved in slow motion. Feeling dizzy, he rubbed his palms together, causing a bright friction – a healing light. He touched his forehead. His lazy eyes became steady. The blisters, bruises, and deep cut on his neck disappeared too.

The bushes glowed. "Prince Elijah!" he remembered. He searched for him, but he realized eventually that he himself caused the glow – his gilded armor and the crystal studs on his boots bathing in daylight. "Come out now! We need to stop the king! The *Chronicles of Light* alone can do it! It contains the *Truth!* Hand over the book! You're done guarding it!" he implored, at length.

The wind blew in. He listened carefully. He heard nothing but the fluttering leaves. He waited. Seconds passed by. It felt like forever. "Don't you want justice for yourself? You were accused of a crime you didn't commit, exiled to this forbidden world!" The veins on his neck popped out in frustration. "A time and a half have passed. Time to go home!" Silence continued. His eyes lighted up. "Oh, I know what you're doing! Quit it, Eli! Stop playing hide and seek! I already grew up!"

Daylight clapped on his face. He turned to the sky and said, "Of course. The sky is our playground." A bitter smile escaped his lips, reminded of his failed take off. He then marshaled his wings and shot up.

Chapter 2: Evergreen

Argos flapped his wings with a flourish. The plain clouds rolled back like scrolls. All the more, he hoped to find the *Chronicles of Light.* The sun cooled down on his wings. His sweltered forehead creased, wondering how the slow time escaped him.

"You took our game way too seriously," he grumbled.

He checked the village below. Nothing glowed from the crowd of lackluster, wingless, snail-paced humans trotting back and forth. He smirked in disgust, his dictionary of them confirmed.

A tiny object slapped him on the face, cutting short his contempt. He looked straight up and realized he failed to yield to a flock of speckled birds flying in V-formation. His hit and run victim lodged a complaint. The rest of the birds squawked in chorus. Afraid to catch attention, he lagged on their tail, pretending he was part of them – migrating.

The spring wind washed him up. Below, the green field ran far and wide. The midget trees swayed. His face crumpled.

"Evergreen thrives with life, while Shadow Lights die each passing night," he said, sinking in self-pity. "Three days left and we'll all be dead. Argh! Why didn't you just hand me the book?" He threw his right fist in the air. "You're wasting time! Our lives are hanging in a balance!

I know you can hear me. You can hear from long ranges. Stop playing deaf!"

The birds squawked. Their throats made a repeated, throbbing noise. Something trickled. His ears wiggled. The flock swerved away to follow the noise. He trailed them, hoping in his heart it had something to do with Prince Elijah. A lackluster man sitting on a bench under a tree tossed seeds on the ground. The birds landed and hungrily ate the seeds. He left promptly, reminded of those *Luceres* who mated with humans and were banished as a result.

"I don't want to live in the dark," he said with a shiver.

Rain poured. He embraced the fall. His wings remained dry. His throat too. He rolled his eyes. It was time for his eye medicine refill. The wind swirled by. His blurry eyes twinkled, catching a familiar scent. Sniffing eagerly, he followed it and ended in front of a secluded two-story, white house with a sprawling lawn. He flashed a knowing smile. He found Prince Elijah's nest! Excited, he surged forward, only to be flung back. An invisible shield blocked him! He soothed his bruised nose; his injured pride too. Turning to the asphalted driveway, he pointed to his shimmering shadow cast on it, quietly arguing his substance. He waited for Prince Elijah to come out and welcome him properly.

Seconds passed.

"What's holding you up?" he wondered, scratching his head.

A vague image of a farm truck sat coldly inside a port. He pulled his head, curious to see one for the first time, and baffled why he used this machine when he could flash in a speed of light. The chimney blew smoke. Unwilling to wait another second, he took another shot. Surging, he crumpled his face. He hit the invisible shield. It disintegrated like a sheer curtain. He heaved a breath of relief. The tarred, winding driveway ushered him in, its color reminding him of the Gray Border. Reaching the house, his wings screeched. The gust shook the rusty gutter.

"Yours was a castle," he mumbled in disgust.

His memory stone blinked. The house turned into a castle with white stucco. The midget trees stood taller and multiplied in number. Like bearing feet, they marched out to encircle the castle. Colorful neon light posts appeared. Rainbow glitters flew – the varied flowers burst with seeds. He swatted the air, catching a handful – his muscle memory at work. His leafy ears wiggled, hearing the water pouring out without content from the white ceramic water basins sprawled across the majestic garden. The golden wing images etched on the wide double front door glimmered. He felt invited. The embedded powdered crystal stones – *healing stones* – sparkled on the white marble porch. His body screamed for rest. While eyeing the stones, hoping to perch, his last sighting of Prince Elijah showed him dancing on the porch.

"Of course! You like dancing in the Great Hall! A great weapon like you!" His broad shoulders shook while he giggled. He then scanned the entire house. His smile faded. Nostalgia hit him. "My family's nest is now in ruins." His eyes squinted. "You were exiled because *he* brought home the battle! *He* ruined your family! *He* tarnished your name! I don't have to tell you the gory details. You have the book!"

The Victorian window shrunk into a tiny bay window. His memory stone ceased. He smirked, disgusted by the house he described looked like a hovel. A light flickered through the window. He eyed it, forcing himself to ignore the ugly façade. He clocked in, assuming the light was Prince Elijah. It stayed in one spot. He grumbled while his shadow grew long against the porch, which he noticed needed serious sanding.

"Stop killing time! We can't afford it!" he shouted.

Dark shadows emerged. Startled, he flew up to the roof. On his way up, he caught a glimpse of the rusty mailbox planted near the landing of the porch. His eyebrows furrowed. "Banner?"

Tiny patters erupted.

He landed gingerly, afraid the flaky roof would collapse. "This can't be an *article's* nest! It can't be. Articles have no military intelligence. Only weapons can put up a defensive shield," he debunked, glancing back at the entrance. "You change your name so you can't be found out!"

Feet rambled. He listened attentively. Three children of different weights were playing; the heaviest was making the floor squeak hard. An adult joined in. His footsteps were careful and tired. His heart jumped.

"You're too slow, Dad!" a boy shouted.

"But it's the slow and steady who wins the race," his father replied.

Argos fell silent. The rasp in his voice was missing! Worse, he incurred the human leg disease! His memory stone blinked. It reminded him how fast Prince Elijah sprinted away from Shadow Lights. His shoulders dropped.

"Your cage became your bliss. You have seeds," he said, adding, "You were bewitched." He blamed the translucent sky. "What is it that you generously offer with your lack?" The sun toned down. "I will remind you of who you are. But you have your memory stone. Unless," he said, pausing. Goosebumps struck. He lifted his ring to his face and promised, "I won't let them look at mine. I won't let these humans control me."

His eye medicine reeked. It wafted from the treed backyard. He took off in frantic flight. The rusty gutter shook. He perched on the closest tree and hid. Three blond heads popped in the window. He held his breath in suspense. Their father pulled them away. His neck elongated, but he only caught a glimpse of him.

"Argh! I need to get my refill the soonest to better see things," he grumbled.

The chimney remained busy. Below it, the kitchen window, a box measuring thirty inches wide and fifty inches high, was open. He pressed his face forward, enjoying the scent squeezed in between the competing smells of boiling mushroom soup and crispy chicken meat swimming inside the Teflon-coated pan. He flew down and snuck up to the window. He peeked in, only to pull back after seeing the back of a woman.

"The human who bewitched Prince Elijah!" he cried.

About to leave, her flowery perfume held him up. He watched her pace back and forth in slow motion. Her long, caramel hair bounced behind her. The color matched her sun-kissed skin. Judging by her appearance, she looked the same age as his mother, about a century old. In a flick, he turned stoic-faced. Her sentiment flashed back. The woman pivoted. She walked toward the window, holding a wooden spatula. He gasped, afraid she would hit him over his contempt. He flashed back to his hiding tree. The crystal studs on his right boot accidentally chipped off bark, making a parallel of long scratches. He tried to push the peeled skin back, fretting about leaving a mark of his presence.

The sky was bathed in red. He fidgeted. Another night. A dark cloud hovered over him. The trees whimpered and turned leprous. Scarlet icicles formed, like beds of snarling snakes. He shushed his blinking memory stone.

The woman opened the window wider. His eye medicine's scent exploded. His mouth watered. On the ground, his shimmering shadow elongated, pointing him toward the house. "My refuge for tonight," he mused, marshaling his wings. For a moment, he hesitated over the size of the window. "It's possible," he said, exhaling sharply before taking a leap of faith. He tripled his speed; his wings clipped tightly. Halfway in through the window, from the corner of his eye, he saw the shadow of the night reach out to him. He panicked, hitting a copper bell hanging on the latch in consequence.

Chapter 3:
The *Gris*

The bell rang.

Feet galloped from the adjacent room. Argos frantically scoured the boxed-in kitchen for a hideout. Distressed white cupboards lined the walls, which were covered with wallpaper bearing a fleur-de-lis design. He squirmed, worried as to when his speed could make him invisible. Shouts rang out. Dark shadows emerged at the doorpost. His glittery form showed up over the tired linoleum floor. Time ticked. His heart jumped. He quickly veered toward the noise. A vintage clock hung in the corner of the room, the only free wall, but it was narrow. He folded his wings behind him tightly and surged toward it with crumpled face. At impact, the wall melted, like a sheer curtain. He entered the musty inner walls clutching his rumbling chest.

Dust trickled like confetti. A sneeze threatened. He pinched his nose to stifle it. It came

out softly. He held his breath in suspense, fearing he stoked them up. Happily, he didn't turn heads. He twisted his body around with strain. The dimmed walls fell on him. He gasped, constricted by the strangled air. The cramped space felt like a coffin – his anxiety speaking. Dust trickled again, his wings bumping against the supporting beams. He covered his mouth and nose with both hands, making sure his sneeze was contained this time.

But worse than his inflamed nose, his tongue itched. A thought came to him.

"I can't wait to report to you the sad news. You'll definitely go beast mode."

Facing the kitchen, he hyperventilated. Four dark shadows slithered toward him. He pulled back and hit a stud. It trembled. He squirmed, afraid they would finally take notice. The front wall stayed calm. He looked at it with interest. The room was insulated. He started breathing easier.

"Ah, finally! I can speak freely!" he sighed.

Tired footsteps drew in. His rheumy eyes ran to the door. The father appeared. His face dropped. He bore the color of a mud! His eyes matched his skin too! Worse, he squirted a farm smell. He quickly panned to the mother.

"What are you doing here? Who are you?" he probed.

The woman turned around. Her bright azure eyes jumped on him.

"A *Gris!*"

Half-*Lucere*, half-human! His eyes widened in shock. "And I thought you were the human-wife of Prince Elijah!" Three pairs of blue eyes joined in. His eyes faltered. "It doesn't compute. Prince Elijah left Shadow Lights about my age!"

"Why did you ring the bell? The dinner isn't ready yet?" a boy grumbled. His loud, raucous voice pierced the wall.

Argos cupped his ears, irritated by his voice. "So, I can hear everything from the outside, but you can't," he figured. "I'm a fly in the wall!"

"Mom pranked us," a girl complained.

The *Gris* squirmed.

"Come now." The father pulled his children away. "Let Mom finish her cooking."

"I'm starving!" The loud boy stomped off.

Dark shadows left. The room lighted up.

Argos exhaled in relief.

By herself, the *Gris* glared at the bell.

"Why are you treating the bell with offense? And where did you get it? That can't be Prince Elijah's. That bell belongs to an article."

He waited for her to speak her thoughts since she wore no memory stone. All she had was a stone-less, inexpensive, gold-plated ring she wore on her ring finger – the weakest finger. He sneered over her frailty but felt dumb expecting much from her, given her complex nature: Heaven and Earth in one body.

She pressed her lips tightly. Her eyes were filled with varied emotions and he couldn't put his finger on them. He started feeling desperate. He yearned to know her thoughts. She held him up in suspense, revealing nothing, until she moved back to the stove.

His mouth watered. On the counter laid a basin of green grapes—his eye medicine. He rubbed his dirty hands, while he calculated the distance. He estimated it should take less than one-eight of a second to grab a piece.

The stirring spatula made a whirring, dull sound. While the *Gris* stirred the cooking soup absently, he leaped out. He reached her spot exactly the way he timed it. He pressed his lips tightly to keep himself from making any noise. When he saw her dark shadow about to touch his feet, he moved back. She stayed oblivious. He then stretched his right arm to the max to grab a stalk while praying in his heart she would stay drifting. About to pluck a piece, she took the basin to the sink. He sank on his feet.

White dust rained. He caught them all. He looked up to the low ceiling and found a parallel of scratches. His wingtips curled in embarrassment. He grumbled quietly. Suddenly, while his attention was on the ceiling, the dripping faucet gained decibels, like a fountain pouring in excess. The worn-out wallpapers turned gilded. The tiny fleur-de-lis design blew up into an enormous damask. The vintage, opaque milk glass ceiling light multiplied into mammoth chandeliers, like clustered stars. The kitchen walls moved back. The white linoleum floor transformed into madacamized white marbles stretching in acres. In the middle of the floor, a huge, gilded pair of wings was stamped.

"The Great Hall," he mused, looking confused.

Merry laughter rang out. From the walls, *Luceres* appeared. They were drinking wine. Their azure eyes sparkled in every sip. He stood among them, feeling out of place with his warrior outfit. They were all dressed fancily—the women wearing gowns and the men wearing expensive fur suits. Their jewelry was lavished, even their wings wore piercings. The women wore heavy make-up, their cheekbones illuminated by a glittery white powder, like the dust in his hands. The orchestra played. Pairs danced.

"The *Celebration of Lights*," he whispered while scouring for their memory stones, looking for a stone identical to his.

A soft breeze touched his cheek.

Dust trickled down on the macadamized floor now fading back into its tired form. The dripping faucet stopped. The walls clamped back and turned ordinary again. The ceiling dimmed. He returned back to his senses. "Now is not the time to look for love," he said, dismayed with himself.

The *Gris* went back to the stove with the basin. He followed her nervously. When she opened the cupboard on top of the stove, he quickly snatched a stalk. He flashed back to his hiding wall. His hands shook with excitement, holding it so fresh. "Finally! Not a pressed fruit! How I wish I can bring some home! They will surely fight over a piece!" he snickered.

Closing his eyes, he quietly gave thanks to Prince Elijah for tilling the forbidden land. His heart tugged. "I'm sorry you became a grassroot. No wonder you smelled like the earth," he said bitterly while recalling the fist-sized ball of light that rescuscitated him from death.

About to eat, he paused briefly, noticing his dirty, untrimmed fingernails. His eyebrows twitched while disposing off the nagging thought that his fate would be like Prince Elijah's. He quickly dunked in the fruits. Scales fell off his eyes. His eyes glowed brightly.

Chapter 4:
The Missing Fruit

"Where are you, Eli? Explain to me how you grew old fast in this slow time? You left Shadow Lights my age, now your seed is older than I am!" Argos grimaced. He felt his head would explode over the disconnect.

Suddenly, a faint light flickered on his left, through the beams.

"Eli!" he shouted.

He started for the light, passing through a maze of beams. His wings fluttered in excitement. His eyes blinked wistful, expecting to see him in the other room reading the *Chronicles of Light*. Reaching the spot, an explosion of amber light greeted him. The setting sun waved goodbye through the bay window in the living room, which he realized was facing the driveway.

"Another day," he mumbled, feeling frantic.

The light faded quickly, revealing an empty, country-styled dining room. A traditional chandelier hung over the table. The glasses twinkled like a mirror ball. He smiled bitterly.

Dark shadows flittered in the living room. His eyes ran toward them. The dividing walls disintegrated. Two dark shadows bounced around, while two other darks shadows watched them from the couch that was pressed against the wall near the window. Clanking noise repeatedly played.

"Where's Eli?" he wondered. "Where's the book?"

A grim feeling swept him. He shook it away. He then waited for him to come down from the second floor of the house; the midget stairs on the right wing he deemed a funny sight. He remained a no-show. His hopes started to skid, but a lonely, midget bookshelf pushed near the stairs saved him. He checked the shelves. It contained children's books, a thick, dog-eared, black, leather Bible, some colorful drawings made by the children, and bundled keys for the house and the truck. He zeroed in on the children's books. "What if Prince Elijah disguised the *Chronicles of Light* as ordinary to keep it safe?" He then closed his eyes, shutting down all noises. The printed words in the books jumped out: Angels; Demons; *Nephelim*. The latter brought him to a smile. He listened again and came across a story.

"Prince Charming? Who's this?" he wondered.

He read a paragraph. "Prince Charming is searching for his true love!" He bolted quickly out of his meditation. Opening his eyes, he was startled by his reflection.

"A mirror!"

His leafy ears stood stiff while he waited for the clock in the kitchen to stop. Impatient and feeling confident, he stepped out of the wall. Suddenly, he felt a presence lurking behind him. He quickly reached for his sword and spun on the balls of his feet. A collection of pictures resting on top of a rustic sideboard confronted him. His pulse quickened; he feared getting pulled into the memories. He remained in the present. A long, sharp exhale escaped his brawny chest. Gathering his courage, he pushed a frame. It tipped over.

"These memories are dead. No wonder they're in these glassed coffins," he mused in disbelief.

He scoured the pictures. One picture showed the *Gris* and her husband on their wedding day. There were pictures celebrating the birth of the children, their baptisms, and birthday celebrations. He noticed an old man was present in all pictures. In one picture he wore a charcoal suit while standing on a pulpit with a Bible in his right hand. In another, he was hugging a woman of the same age, probably his wife. There was something special about him he couldn't put his finger on with his salt and peppered hair, tired, honey-wheat eyes, crumpled skin riddled with condemned valleys and age spots.

"Ah, the human's father," he said, comparing their eyes.

He scanned him for the last time. About to turn away, he caught a glimpse of his diamond ring. His memory stone blinked. It recognized the stone.

"Why do you have Prince Elijah's stone?" His face paled. "If you have it, then it means he's… dead."

The memory of Prince Elijah crossing the Gray Border flashed back. He realized it was just the witness stones in the Omniscient Gate showing him who crossed last. He glared at the picture, now wishing he could enter it.

"If I can find your memory stone, then I can find the book! Not only the book, but a treasure chest of memory stones! Power! Knowledge! Secrets!" he exclaimed, catching his breath in excitement. "Who would have thought I'd be getting a windfall for doing the forbidden? But, where is it? It should be here, otherwise, you won't put that protective sensor up for nothing!"

The clock ticked. He gasped. Time didn't stop. He quickly panned to the living room, then to the kitchen. He gripped his sword, just in case. No one moved from their spots. Relieved, he flashed back to the wall.

The living room floor squeaked with grinding feet. A loud thud erupted, followed by a pained groan.

"Ouch!" a boy whimpered.

"Be careful, *Eli!*" the father admonished.

"Eli?" Argos quickly went to the living room. He passed through the cramped, musty, darkened maze of bricks, not minding the trickling dust. He mouthed Eli's name repeatedly while closing in, deeply curious about who owned the name that he could still hear being whispered like a prayer inside the city.

Reaching the living room, he positioned himself behind the old, sleeping fireplace on the wall, to the right of the bay window. His curious eyes roamed. A vintage, high-back chair was pressed against the window. Beside it stood an oak side table. A bitter smile escaped his lips. He imagined Prince Elijah reading the *Chronicles of Light.*

The owl hooted. He turned to the window on his left. Herds of dark clouds ran peacefully on errands, leaving ample space for the stars and the moon. His eyes blinked wistful, recalling cruising the pale moonlight with his friends; their varied memory stones making rainbows. Musical instruments serenaded the night—strumming guitars and blowing wind instruments. The music was gentle to the spirit, very unlike the clanging noise at hand. The walls reverberated. Dust trickled. He clamped his nose. When the dust settled, he pulled his head out, and was shocked to see a mock battle in progress.

"I tried and I'm already tired!" the stout, loud boy complained. "Who gave you the authority to change the game anyway?" The plastic sword in his grip almost slipped out of his sweaty palm.

"I'm older than you. For the record!" the skinny one insisted in his stentorian voice; his back facing the wall.

Argos rolled his eyes. "I don't want to be the secret jury to this lame game!" he protested. Still, he couldn't help himself not to watch. "Because it's the first time I saw your kind," he excused. "Plus, this wall allows me to speak to you safely," he added, glancing at his memory stone with a look of relief. "So, here's my verdict. If you boys get into a real scrap, you," he said, pointing to the younger brother, "can pin him down easily," he continued, turning his finger to the eldest. He then noticed their clothes. "Why did you swap clothes?" he asked, making a face-palm.

The younger brother wore a skin-tight shirt, which gave him red marks on his arms; the sleeves were like cuffs meant to restrain him. The eldest swam inside his oversized shirt, which flapped like a banner against his frail frame. Their copper-blond hair and sun-kissed skin stopped his poor appraisal. He shrank back, embarrassed by his anemic skin. When the boys switched places, his jaws dropped. The eldest wore thick eyeglasses!

"I don't want to play anymore, *Eli!*" The younger brother dropped his sword.

Argos lost the color on his face, drained by utter shock. "This boy is named so well to have poor eyes!" Upset, he clawed his dirty fingers against him, wanting to strip him of the honor. He zoomed in on his radiant blue eyes muted by his spectacles, blaming it for his sour attitude. "Your eyes are poor that's why you can't see the plain truth right before you! Your arrogance makes me vomit!" he lambasted. "Prince Elijah never rested on his birthright! He was never an overlord despite the red-carpet treatment afforded him! Had not the black book intervened, he would have been the king! But you, an adulterated version, a skinny overlord with weak eyes and dark shadow!" He suddenly paused, tasting the words he just spilled in head. "If only Prince Elijah imposed his birthright just like what you're doing, then lives would have been spared. Families would still be complete. Shadow Lights would remain glorious." His belittling eyes softened.

"Eli wants to be a knight," the little girl said, disrupting his thoughts. She spoke in a whisper but she managed to stir him up for she spoke with emphasis, as if sharing vital information. "Harold wants the same," she added with raised left eyebrow, obviously doubting his capacity.

Argos sneered. "Harold sounds like *Herald.* No wonder he's loud."

"You are a knight too," her father replied.

"I'm not!" she refused, shaking her head vigorously. "I have no weapon!"

"You do have a weapon: your *eyes.*"

The brothers chortled.

"That's not funny, Dad," she grumbled, crossing her arms over her chest.

He kissed her gently on the head. Her grumpy eyes calmed down.

Eli struck Harold on the chest.

"Mom!!!" Harold cried out, twisting his body toward the kitchen. His flab mounted.

"Do you always have to report everything?" Eli rebuked in a controlled voice, not wanting her meddling.

"Harold's a tattletale!" The little girl made a bird beak with her mouth.

Harold faced her with his sword leveled against her elfin face. "Stick and stones may break my bones, but your words will never hurt me!" he declared, squinting his puppy eyes.

"Not in my world!" Argos countered, somehow caught in the middle. "Our spoken words are mightier than the finest sword! It hurts! It kills! The king read a spell from the black book and it destroyed our land!"

"Come on! Catch me off-guard!" Eli demanded.

Harold walked away. "I give up! I can't catch up!"

"When you come to the end of your rope, tie a knot and hang on," the father instructed.

"Who said that?" Harold asked.

"Franklin D. Roosevelt."

His daughter yanked his sleeve. "Who is he?"

"He was the thirty-second president of the United States."

Eli scowled. "Dad! You're speaking about *politics* over our small family game!"

"There's politics everywhere. Even in families, I tell you."

"Politics in families, true in every word!" Argos clenched his jaws.

Harold secretly picked up his sword. He craftily snuck up on Eli's blind side.

Argos leaned forward, feeling a sudden adrenaline rush. He wanted to step out as his stone went back to the past, to that single time he rushed to Prince Elijah's nest to give him a head's up. Wings geared up, he opened his mouth, but the words remained in his head.

Harold hit Eli on the back.

"What the…?" Eli flinched.

"*Yaaaay*!! I just hit your HEART! I tied the score, but I WON!" Harold jumped up and down.

The floor squeaked hard.

Argos made a face-palm. "Yesterday and today, I'm still late."

"But that's a *cheat!*" Eli whined.

"Nope. That's a *trick!*" Harold clarified.

"Nobody wins by *tricking!*"

Argos's eyes blazed in anger. "Tell that to the king! Tell that cheat! He invited the *Umbra* to cover up his misdeeds!" The thick herds of dark clouds cloaking the glittery sky in Shadow Lights flashed back in his mind. He shivered in fear. "But he will be found out soon!" His dusty palms itched. He wanted to snatch Eli and fly him to Shadow Lights and let him bring the truth-words he just uttered to power. "Tell him again," he prodded. "Tell your brother."

Harold bowed, about to exit the game; his girth the size of a bread loaf. "You cannot fight me anymore. You're bleeding to death. I just crushed your heart! GAME OVER!" He made a running man dance on his way to the couch, causing the floor to squeak again.

"You will destroy this house," his sister said.

Harold blew raspberries.

Eli grumbled. "You can't do that! I'm still alive!" he contested, pressing his right index against his bony chest.

"Yu-uh! I killed you already. What? Did you just REINCARNATE?" Harold laughed with sarcasm.

Argos glared at Eli. "By virtue, you are indeed his resurrection since you have his name. But you have poor eyes!"

Chapter 5:
Bewitched

"What's *reincarnate*?" asked their sister.

"It means a dead person who came back to life again," her father answered in the same puzzled tone.

"Oh. Is that even possible?"

"Well, no."

"Then why did Harold say that?"

"Well, let's just say, you are a reincarnation of Mom because you look like her!"

"Oh, I get it now!"

Argos caught their talk. He glanced her way. She sat anonymous all this time. Upon scrutiny, he realized she possessed a heart-shaped face, aquiline nose, full lips with smiley sides and radiant almond eyes. "She looked very much like a *Lucere*," he observed.

"*Lucy* does look like Mom," Eli agreed.

"What a beautiful name! Lucy short for *Luceres*!" Argos stuck his right thumb up.

Sparks flew. He ducked, surprised by the mini-fireworks clapping over his head. He panned back to Lucy. His eyes turned whimsical. She morphed into a beautiful, grown woman!

The moonlight peered in. Her sun-kissed skin sparkled under its light. Her long, sandy blond hair shimmered, smoothed with the finest oil. He took a deep breath, filling his chest with her scent. He briefly glanced at his blinking memory stone and saw his reflection. He looked every inch enchanted. His conscience prompted him to steer away, but he couldn't take his eyes off her. She looked so feline and fragile.

"I won't break your heart and prick you to tears," he promised, his voice with a lilt.

The flower designs on the couch sprouted to life. They shot up over her head, like fancy umbrellas, and spurted sparkly, colorful seeds. A handful crawled like furry animals on her lap. His chest mounted, pumped up with large dosages of hope. "We are a perfect match! A weapon should be paired with someone who adores the flowers. Yes! Bring forth hope amid the turmoil!"

He shivered, plagued with a sweet fever rushing all over him. His leafy ears wiggled, hearing his heart palpitate, playing a sweet tune. The high walls he set up around it crumbled; he compared its shaking to the shaking ground from last night. Gazing steadfastly at her beautiful face, he enshrined every bit of it. She smiled at him. He felt invited. He geared up, longing to embrace her naked body in desperate need to be dressed with his light. But when he looked past her, she had no wings! He rapidly put his wings to a screeching stop, halting his forbidden desire. Dust trickled like rain. His wings stirred uncomfortably. He threw his right hand in the air, disowning the vision of love. Lucy morphed back to her tiny size, a child again. The moon moved back. The flowers on the couch wilted. The clapping sparks vanished. He clutched his chest hard, seized with a panic attack.

"I already warned you about humans. Even without speaking spells, they enchant!" His mother's warning boomed out from his memory stone.

He exhaled sharply, glad her words followed him. "No! I won't get bewitched like Father! I refuse this spell! This can't be my fate! I will not ask a human to marry me!" he blasted.

"I do," Lucy said in a singsong.

He quickly covered his memory stone, afraid she read his thoughts.

"Ey! You bested Eli for the first time. It never happened in the past!" she said in disbelief. "Eli always ruled!"

Harold clicked his tongue. "Time has changed in my favour."

"You should play by the *rules!*" Eli contended.

"Bah! Give it a rest! It's just a game!" Feeling complacent, Harold laid his back against the cushions, placed his feet up on the coffee table and clasped his hands under his head.

Eli gathered the swords. "Listen to yourself," he fumed. "We're just playing and you can't play fair!" He dragged his feet on his way to the toy bin in the foyer, sending Harold into a mocking titter.

Argos watched Eli carry the swords to the foyer. "Prince Elijah's sword!" he suddenly remembered. "Where is it? The book, his memory stone and his sword – all missing!"

The *Gris* showed up. She looked exactly like Lucy's future self. He then remembered the other seeds. "They must be beautiful too!" he quipped, but he backpedaled promptly. He slapped his right cheek, punishing himself for reaching that place of admiration.

"Help me set up the table, *Noah*," she requested.

"Noah?" His crossing the Gray Border flashed back. "The *Great Flood*," he nervously mused while zeroing in on the Bible. He started in the book of Genesis, flipping the pages with his eyes until he reached chapter seven.

"All the underground waters erupted from the earth, and the rain fell in mighty torrents from the sky," he read with heaviness. "The good books recorded the same event. Heavy rains flooded the earth, but Noah made an ark and survived. Fear and dread fell on every beast and on every surviving Nephelims on his account. The *Patriarchs* sacrificed their memory stones to build the Gray Border – seven stones in all. Its united colors showed up in the sky, a rainbow, before it plunged into the chasm, along with the beasts of the earth. We lived in peace in Shadow Lights after that," he narrated, at length.

Noah stood up from his rest.

Argos bowed before him by reflex. "This human might be of great character, otherwise, Prince Elijah won't give his daughter's hand. He must have seen a glimpse of light in his body of darkness," he said, trembling.

"Sure, Stella!" Noah replied.

"Stella means star!" Argos felt a tug in his heart. His eyes mellowed. "Prince Elijah named her accordingly. She is a light surrounded by a world full of darkness. Just like her nature – lightness and darkness in one body," he reasoned. As they moved away, he looked on, filled with envy. She coiled her right hand around Noah's left arm, as if going to a dance. The love connection between them was evident.

Eli returned from the foyer. His eyes squinted. "Hey, King Harold! You took my spot!"

"Mine now!" Harold wiggled his right index in the air.

"Boys, keep it down," Lucy admonished while her eyes panned to Stella, who returned with a rustic, golden candelabra with three lighted white candles in it. She placed the candelabra on the fireplace mantel.

Argos sniffed its glow thirstily. He smiled and said, "My candle of life remained aglow."

The moment Stella left, Eli pursued his argument. "You tricked me!" he growled at Harold, sticking his bony index finger at his face.

"You just can't handle the *truth!*" Harold smirked.

"Where is the *Truth*?" Argos fussed.

Lucy whipped her right hand in the air, pretending to catch a flying insect. She then crumpled her fist and moved it close to Eli's mouth. "Eat it," she offered, opening it slowly. "It's the *truth:* You lost to Harold for the first time!"

Eli looked at her frostily. "I'm not eating that lie!" he refused, pushing her hand away.

"Aw! You spilled the truth! What a waste!" she moaned, her shoulders dropping.

"Don't put words into my mouth!" he rebuked, adding, "Besides, that's a lie! Lies taste

bad in my mouth!"

Harold's eyes narrowed. "Lucy told the truth! Liar!"

"Liar, liar! Your eyes on fire!" Lucy teased, sticking her right index in his eyes.

Eli swatted her hand. "You're poking fun at my eyes again!" he barked, sinking in self-pity.

"Yeah! Your bangs are reaching your eyes! That's why your *eyes* are on fire!" she pursued, giving him a stink eye.

"Eli is a liar," Harold pressed, irritating him further.

"I said quit it! Right now!" Eli demanded.

Argos watched him squirm over their allegation. His nostrils were flaring, his thin lips pressed against each other, his round eyes thinking, obviously concocting a plan to salvage his name. He sneered. "You are not worthy of it," he pointed out. By accident, his right wingtip stuck out. He pulled it back at once when he felt a pair of eyes steely gazing at him—Eli's! He moved back, feeling mixed emotions from shock to wonder.

The copper bell rang.

The children raced to the dining table.

Chapter 6:
Lightning and Thunder Equal Injustice

Argos beat them. "If indeed he saw me, then he can find the *Chronicles of Light!*" he rejoiced from behind the mirror. "I want to see it again. I will test his gift of sight."

"I'm back!" Eli shouted, throwing his fists up in the air, feeling victorious "I'm so back in the game! The score is tied!" He tapped the table, shaking the utensils.

"Eli, don't touch the grapes yet," Stella warned from the kitchen.

Noah laughed softly. "That's his favorite," he mused.

"Promise, I won't." Eli sat down, his eyes set on the grapes.

Argos pulled his head. "Then why do you still have poor eyes?" But he remembered he did see him.

Harold plopped his heavy weight against the chair on Eli's right. "Huh? How can you race when you're already dead?" he argued.

"I was reincarnated, remember?" Eli tapped his right temple.

"Oomph! Even if I have quick feet, I won't win!" Lucy grumbled on her way to the farthest seat, the one backing the mirror.

"That too!" Harold agreed.

Eli sneered. "Duh! Seriously? You both think I won because my chair is closest to the living room? Nu-uh! I'm the eldest that's why I sit on Dad's right!"

Noah stepped in from the kitchen with his wet hands up; his lumberjack polo and khaki pants bearing tiny splatters of mud stains. "I heard my name." He stood confused for a moment. "Oh, I get it. It's the race," he realized shortly after. "Well, since Eli sat first, then he will lead the grace," he instructed, earning groans of protest from Harold and Lucy. He sat across from Lucy, in full view of Argos.

Eli pressed his face against Harold and shouted, "You heard Dad!"

"Ouch! You don't need to scream in my ear!" Harold cupped his ears.

"*Dumbo* has sensitive ears!" Eli sniggered.

Harold shoved him on the shoulder. "Don't call me Dumbo, *Mr. Bright Eyes!"* he fired back, wiping the smugness off his face. "Secondly, it is not me who is *sensitive!*" he continued, giving Lucy a side-eye.

"Nu-uh! Don't drag me in your fight!" she countered, wiggling her right index in the air.

Argos narrowed his eyes. "I will drag you all into our fight if I don't find the book!" he shouted while glaring against the family. He then zeroed in on Eli. Itching to prove he has the gift of sight, he rubbed his hands excitedly, producing a soft beam of light that he rolled like a piece of clay.

"I'm hot," Lucy gushed suddenly, fanning her right hand over her blushed cheeks.

Argos quickly stopped rubbing his palms, upset he had misfired.

Harold scoffed. "LOL! You're not *hot* at all," he said, stifling his contemptuous giggle. "You're just a random girl."

"LOL? What is this code?" Argos scratched his head.

"Just take a bath!" Eli laughed.

"Oh, I will! I'll even make a double dip in the Purification Lake!" Argos hollered. He folded his wings forward, like a fur coat, and smoothed his wings. His eyes mellowed. "I will lose this fullness in that sweltering purge!"

Lucy complained, "Why are you on me? You were at odds a while ago, and now you're a team and I'm your target!"

Noah jumped in. "Okay, enough of this argument. Whenever you have your disagreements, you know the *rule*," he said, swaying his hands in the air, like a conductor of an orchestra.

"*Love* covers all wrongs," they all chorused in with a lilt.

Argos nodded. "Words to live by," he approved. "How does this silver fox know?"

Stella stepped in from the kitchen carrying a bowl of hot soup. She placed it in the center of the table like it was the main entree. The family rubbed their hands. There were boiled sweet corns, fried chicken, mashed potato, and grapes.

"Grassroot fare," Argos described smugly.

Lucy noticed an extra plate on her right. "Are we expecting any visitor?" she asked Stella.

Argos's stomach grumbled.

Stella shrugged. "Dad set the table."

Noah raised his right hand. "Guilty as charged."

Eli glanced at the extra plate, then smiled. "Well, who knows there'll be an additional family member in the future," he exclaimed, prompting Noah and Stella to pull their heads back.

"Oh, yeah!" Harold shouted, throwing his clenched right fist in the air in celebration.

Stella shook her head vigorously. "No! You three are already a handful! Why did you even come up with that, Eli?"

"I just thought, maybe —"

"Can you see the *future?*" Noah laughed.

Argos squinted his eyes. "He will! If he finds the book!"

"Maybe that's the reason why he's *farsighted!*" Lucy giggled aloud.

"Not funny!" Eli gave her a black look.

Stella turned serious. "By the way, have you heard of Mrs. Whiteburn's sudden death?" she asked Noah.

Noah nodded solemnly. "No wonder her stall in the market is closed. I thought she and Mr. Whiteburn went on a trip. How did you know?" he asked.

"A little birdie told me." Her eyes flitted toward the mirror.

Argos panicked. "Can you see me too?"

Stella casually looked away.

Lucy moaned. "Aw. I'm so sorry to hear Mr. Whiteburn's loss."

"You mean, his *losses*," Eli intoned with meaningful eyes. "He had married three times you know. For the record."

"OMG!" Harold covered his mouth.

Argos rolled his eyes. "Not another code!"

Stella noticed Noah's downcast face. "Okay, change the topic now," she implored.

"Dad remembers his dead dad," Lucy revealed. "Grandpa, I mean."

Argos panicked. "If he's dead too, where is Prince Elijah's memory stone?"

"Well, death is not the greatest loss in life." Noah heaved a sigh.

"Then what is it?" Eli inquired.

"The greatest loss is what dies inside us while we still live," he preached, resting his right hand over his tanned, brawny chest.

"*Love*," Stella answered.

Noah turned to Stella. His left hand searched for hers. "Love doesn't die. Death can't kill it. We carry it with us forever," he exhorted with whimsical voice as if serenading her. "Love knows no bounds. No death, distance, time, race, or differing tongues can stop it from spreading its wings inside our hearts. It bridges the world," he continued, stroking his thumb against her skin.

Argos listened to Noah's heartbeat. His heart was pumping with huge doses of *Love*, the middle fruit! "No wonder that's all he's been talking about. His mouth speaks what's in his heart," he said, feeling melancholic. "I have never heard such loud love vibrations! I never saw Father look at Mother this way." His eyes squinted. "I blame that human!" The candles on the fireplace sizzled out. His countenance changed. "I need to save Father!"

"Wow! That's deep," Harold enthused. "So poetic!"

"I got it!" Eli claimed.

"You, young man, have an old head on your young shoulders," Stella praised.

"Maybe that's why he's wearing thick eyeglasses," Lucy jeered.

"Don't start on me, *Cry Me a River* doll!" he told her off.

Harold's stomach grumbled. "I'm hungry," he shyly admitted, eliciting soft chortles around him.

"You really find a way to be heard, Harold!" Eli tickled his plump brother.

"Stop!" Harold pushed his hand away.

"Eli," Noah called out, gesturing his right hand toward the table.

Argos took a deep breath, then started toward Eli's spot. "It's playtime!" he said, rubbing his hands together.

"Game on!" Eli declared, clasping his hands. "I'm the *hero* for the night!" he bragged, prompting Harold to frown. About to close his eyes, he caught a glimpse of the prying, full moon outside the kitchen window. He smiled. The spotlight was on him. "Dear God," he began with an impish smile. "Thank You for the food. Bless the loving hands of my Mom. She prepared all these for us because she loves us so much and *equally*," he continued, nudging Harold's left elbow, making him wince softly. "May we be nourished, strengthened…" He paused, feeling a warm bite on his nape.

Argos giggled. The hairs on his nape bristled. His skin was red as an apple. He pushed his right glowing hand further, burning his skin all the more.

"Ouch," Eli cried.

Argos pulled back.

The heat dissipated.

Eli snorted, smelling something minty. "Vicks?" he wondered. He quickly leaned against Harold, about to smell his left arm.

Argos shot up from the wall, passing through his left side while his face was on Harold. He made quick trips around the table, then returned back to his original spot, behind the mirror.

Eli froze like a deer in the headlights. The metal frame of his eyeglasses glinted, touched by the blazing trail Argos left behind. "Lightning?"

Harold's stomach grumbled. It sounded like thunder in his ears.

The bright chandelier swayed. Eli lifted his face and eyed the twinkling lights, convincing himself it was all he saw.

"Eli," Noah called out softly, startling him for a moment. "Finish the grace."

Eli clasped his hands again. "A-and… healed. May You never cease to bless us too," he prayed, trying to keep his voice on an even keel.

Suddenly, he felt the warm, prickly thing on his nape again. Beads of sweat formed on his forehead and upper lips. He opened his eyes promptly, grabbing the chance while everyone was oblivious. He snorted. The minty scent lingered. He turned to the kitchen window. "Maybe Mom planted a eucalyptus and the wind is blowing its scent in," he whispered, trying to make sense.

A light flickered on the right side of his face.

"*Eli…*"

Eli's face turned pale. *Who are you?* he wanted to ask the unfamiliar male voice, but he couldn't find his voice. The tips of his hair glowed like a spotlight was on him. It wasn't the moon. "It's the lightning," he gasped.

Argos contained his giggles. Eli looked enchanted, but he gathered himself quickly. His face told him he was dismissing him as a sheer fantasy. He scratched his chin, intrigued by the way he processed things.

Eli bowed his head again, resolved it would be the last time he'd be doing it.

Argos stepped out. He sliced the air, hitting the bottom of the chandelier. His eyes became like saucers, seeing him up-close. Broad forehead hidden beneath his long bangs, round, brilliant eyes muted by his thick eyeglasses, thin lips, and heart-shaped face, he was Prince Elijah's dead ringer! When he saw his eyes in his reflection, he smiled in satisfaction. While hovering over the table, he plucked a piece of grape before heading to the adjacent living room.

Eli pulled back, causing his chair to tip backward.

Everyone opened their eyes.

"What's wrong?" Noah asked.

"He's stalling," Lucy alleged.

Harold glowered at him.

Eli fidgeted, rooted to the spot. "Er, I saw something bright, like um, lightning. It flashed to the living room!" he squeaked with flared nostrils.

"Oh, dear!" Stella covered her mouth, shocked by his tale, and worse, by her reaction.

Noah stood up and went to the living room. He returned shortly with a bewildered face. "The front door is locked. I make sure each night," he implied.

Stella handed Eli a napkin. "Wipe your face," she dotingly commanded. Her wary eyes wandered toward the living room.

Eli took the napkin and used it to take cover from Harold and Lucy's questioning eyes.

"Why are you breaking out in a cold sweat?" Noah looked on worried.

Eli panned his face toward the kitchen.

"Elijah!" Noah called out.

"W-what?" Eli asked, surprised he called him by his first name.

"Do you have fever?"

"I-I don't have fever, but I really did see a bright light flashed over there!" His voice cracked in frustration.

"Well, if it's a bright light then it must be Rev. Goodfellow's car," Stella assumed, diffusing the tension. "You see, he arrives at this time of day."

"Most likely," Noah agreed. He tried to lock eyes with Eli, but he dodged his effort. "Now, finish your prayer so we can all eat dinner. The food is getting cold."

Harold clasped his hands angrily. "Jeez. I'm really hungry! Finish it, will you!"

Eli breathed a deep sigh. He clasped his hands and shyly prodded them to follow along. "B-bless this food so that —"

Argos appeared from the wall between Eli and Harold, munching the grape. His eyes glowed. He bent toward Eli's right ear, implanting him with inaudible words. His ears wiggled, hearing Harold snorting, smelling his scent. He quickly hid again, excited to see the next scene unfold.

Eli's eyes fluttered proudly, rehearsing the words in his mind. About to declare his closing words, Harold cut him off. "So that we may be ready to serve those who are in need of help."

"Amen!" Everyone opened their eyes.

Argos dropped his jaws. "Harold has the gift of hearing!"

Stella lighted up. "That was a very good closing prayer," she praised Harold who shrugged flamboyantly.

"You stole my thunder," Eli barked under breath.

Harold sniggered. His cherubic cheeks mounted like big lollipops. "LOL! You told me to say it after you so I did," he claimed, startling him. Turning to the food, he rubbed his hands excitedly. "Yay! Finally!"

Eli's nostrils flared. "Trickster," he whispered.

"Nu-uh!" Harold shook his head.

"Yes, you are! You won the sword game by deceit and now you rounded up the grace," he retaliated with controlled voice, not wanting to earn his parent's reprimand.

"Watch out!" Stella warned, lifting the lid off the hot soup.

Steam rose up. Eli noticed moisture built up on the mirror. "Smokes and mirrors," he said, mainly to himself.

Harold elbowed him and said, "What's wrong with you? You're out of line."

Eli wanted to rebuke him for eavesdropping again, but he couldn't. "Just pinch me," he requested softly.

"Pinch you? For what?"

"To wake me up."

"Wake you from what?"

"Okay. If you don't want to pinch me then punch me."

"Sounds like a good opportunity, but why will I put myself in trouble when I'm now the *hero* of the night?" he pointed out, making a meaningful glance at his parents. "I'm *more* than okay. Thanks to you."

Eli pretended he heard none of what he said. He let his frightful eyes do the loud, nervous blathering.

Harold watched him with contempt. "Seriously, get a hold of yourself," he advised, adding, "And when you're done with your *fantasy*, please find Eli. His *light* went to the living room."

"I'm not a dim-wit, dim-wit!" he blasted, only to refrain after Stella handed his bowl of soup.

"It's good the soup is still hot," she said, giving him a concerned look.

"Yay! My all-time favorite—mushroom soup!" Noah exclaimed gleefully, altering the tensed mood over the table. "There's a secret ingredient to this only Mom knows."

"What is it?" Lucy wondered.

"*Love!*" he declared, clutching his chest tight as if having a heart attack.

Lucy and Harold shared giggles.

Eli kept mum. He lowered his face and was shocked to see the grapes missing a stem.

Chapter 7:
Copy the Moon

Time ticked slowly, like a funeral tolling bell.

"I know it's morning already in Shadow Lights!" Argos grumbled at the clock hanging above the doorpost in the boys' shared bedroom.

Eli sat frozen on his bed. His skinny legs crossed and his frail body swam inside his green jammies with star imprints. He stared vacantly against the foot of the wall facing his bed where Argos hid. His shallow cheeks bore concentration marks.

"You're brain-fried. I tasered you with my glow. I just, um, had to test your eyes," Argos said, feeling remorseful. "But hey, look up! Come on! This is the best time to talk! We're alone!" he prodded with a hand gesture.

The door flung wide. Lucy barged in carrying a colorful book he wished was the disguised *Chronicles of Light.* She sat in front of him, blocking his view. He rolled his eyes, deeming her a constant distraction.

Clinked.

Blackout!

Argos jolted. "*Umbra!*"

Eli and Lucy vanished from their spots.

A bulky dark shadow rushed in. The empty bed near the closet squeaked.

"Harold," Argos figured. He watched his silhouette reach for the custom-made lampshade with bird cut-outs sitting on the bedside table squished in between their single beds. The lamp started spinning. On the upper right corner of the room, near the clock, a light glowed. It took shape, multiplied, and started spinning in a merry-go-round.

"Time for *bird-watching!*" Harold shouted.

The room began to illuminate dimly. Eli reappeared with his face now tilted toward the ceiling. Lucy changed her spot. She sat on his right clutching the book to her chest. Her short legs dangled on the edge of the bed; her ankles bore a farmer's tan. He smiled timidly, glad she gave him a clear view.

"Please, Eli." Lucy tugged his sleeve.

Argos smiled wryly, partly glad she called him out and partly dismayed she always acted out what he planned to do.

Eli blinked as if awakened. He turned to her and asked, "Are you on the *lookout* too?" But he backed away sheepishly after seeing the book on her lap. "I don't have energy to read for you."

Harold smirked. "Gosh, Lucy! I thought you'd notice the cue and leave!" he shouted, waiving his hand.

Lucy gave him a side-eye. "I'm not here for you, FYI," she rebutted, panning back to Eli. "So, how does this *lightning*, rather this *'talking mini-comet,'* sound like?" she whispered, earning snickers from Harold.

Argos narrowed his eyes. "I'm a talking mini-comet?"

Eli's cheeks blushed. "I know I cooked the perfect recipe for your fantasy, Lucy, but please go to your room. I'm not going to feed your curiosity," he said; his shy eyes prodding her toward the door.

Lucy shook her head hard. "Nope. I'm staying! If you don't speak it out, it will eat you up!" she lectured, tapping her right temple. "I'm just helping you out."

"I'm not sick in mind! So, lay off me!" he pleaded, pushing her on the shoulder. She almost tipped over, but he caught her in time. "I'm sorry. But seriously, if you want to help, just don't ask me to relive it again. Besides, I'm still trying to figure it out," he continued; his words trailed off.

Lucy moved back to her original spot, blocking Argos's view again.

Harold threw a mild fit. His bed shook. "There's nothing to figure out! Go out, Lucy! You're not welcome here!"

Lucy shushed him.

"But Eli doesn't want to remember!"

Argos wiggled his right index in the air. "No! Let him remember! Let's see what he digs up in his memory stone, I mean, memory bank," he said, correcting himself. "It might be useful. A clue!" When Eli's eyes drifted, his eyes widened in interest. "Spill it!"

"He's back!" Eli nervously declared.

"Who?" Lucy asked, startled by his tone.

Harold flipped to his left, suddenly interested.

"R-remember that hunky *albino* in a dark hood I saw in the marketplace?" Eli stammered. "That ultra-bright skinned, faceless man..."

"Oh, the ring thief!" Lucy remembered.

Eli nodded his head like a bobblehead doll. "Yes! Yes! It's him! He alone can pull that flawless trick! I-I took my eyes off him in a split second and he was swoosh!" he claimed, pushing his left hand in the air, toward the window. "But why would he come here and make a repeat of his trick?"

Argos panicked. "An albino in dark hood? Could it be a *Deorc* crossed before me? He must have found Prince Elijah's memory stone! His sword and the *Chronicles of Light* too!" He fidgeted, not knowing what to do.

"That's impossible!" Harold flipped back to his amusement.

"Right?" Argos agreed, gesturing his left hand toward him. "The warlords are still asleep!"

Harold continued. "The doors were locked. Dad made sure! There was no intruder!" He rolled his eyes. "I thought the 'old head on young shoulders' will finally talk with sense!"

"Then who was it, *Dumbo*?" Eli fired back.

"I think *Mom* already explained what you saw," he maintained.

"That can't be Reverend Goodfellow's car's headlight," he refuted.

Lucy crossed her arms across her chest. "Well, I'm not going anywhere yet! We need to sift this through!"

"Geez, Lucy! You are really *hot*—as in pestering, blistering, annoying!" Harold clawed his fingers against her.

"Touch me and I will scream," she warned.

"Eli! Can you please call your *comet?* I want her out of the room NOW!" he fumed.

Eli grabbed his extra pillow and hurled it at him, hitting him in the face. "Cut me some slack, cheater! You pulled a fast one in our sword game, then the grace!" he accused.

The pillow boomeranged to his face.

Harold stood up from his rest, causing the bed to squeak again. "I know you don't like being a loser for once!" he countered. "I saw a bright light flash in the living room. Oh, and yeah, this light, he called my name!" he mimicked sarcastically.

Eli lowered his head. "That's the truth even if it's hard to believe," he insisted meekly. Upset, he clenched his fists and thumped his bed, throwing off Lucy.

"Don't stretch it out. Arf! Arf!" Harold made an angry dog shadow.

"Truth will out, I swear," Eli promised to himself.

"I wonder why he knows your name." Lucy tapped her chin mindlessly.

"Must be a ghost from the past!" Harold laughed.

"Keep quiet, Harold!" she rebuked nervously. "There's no such thing!"

"Hah! Tell him about it!" Harold tittered mockingly.

Eli shook his head, feeling helpless convincing him.

Lucy turned to her book. Her eyes moved, then she smiled timidly. "Who knows that albino was actually a disguised prince who came from a distant place. He saw a princess dressed in rags and he fell in love with her," she proposed.

"This isn't about *love*, Lucy," Eli opposed. "I'm after the *truth*!" he continued, earning a strong nod of approval from Argos.

Lucy continued. "Two lovers, coming from two different worlds – it's the perfect love story!"

Eli shook his head. "Don't forget, that albino is a thief!" he reminded, dousing her fancy. "Why do you think of such? You're too young to think of love!"

"It's your fault!" Harold blamed. "Your bedtime stories suck! That's why she's always away with her fairies!"

"Uh-uh!" Lucy wiggled her tiny, right index finger in the air. "Cinderella is a good story. It's about true love and there's *justice* in the end," she argued, adding, "You're just negative 'coz you don't glow. Nobody has a crush on you."

"Glow? Crush?" Harold retorted. "Do you listen to the words coming out from your lips? Girl, you're still young! Stop this nonsense!"

"You don't know a thing about *love*," she fired back, turning her back against him.

"And you know so much because you have a boyfriend! Yeah, I get it. Your boyfriend is imaginary. LOL!"

Lucy placed the book on Eli's lap. "Switch on the light and read for me please," she begged in a demanding tone.

Eli returned her book. "Not tonight," he refused, wearied out by her persistence.

"Please," she begged, clasping her hands together. "I can't sleep if you don't read for me."

Harold volunteered. "Oh, I will read for you! Let me!"

Lucy cast a skeptical eye. "Are you for real?"

Harold cleared his throat. "And when that rich prince kissed the *Annoying Princess of Evergreen,* that is you," he said with modulated voice; his left hand gesturing toward her, "Tadah! She turned into a scaredy cat!"

"You're too loud!" she exploded, loathing his narrative.

"It's because the *speaker* is huge," Eli sneered, glancing at his flabby girth.

"And why did you twist the story?!" she continued, seething.

Harold grinned. "Why? Don't you like it *dark?* Every story has a villain and a curse! A dark spell!"

Argos's wings fluttered nervously. "The black book! It came back, hence this war! But wait," he paused, pondering. "What if Prince Elijah covered the *Chronicles of Light* with a spell?" He panned back to Eli, feeling a hunch. "He gave you his name not empty of purpose.

With all your demerits, no one would think of you as his heir! You're not a threat! What a smart military tactic! The book will listen to you!"

Eli checked the time. "It's past nine already, Lucy. Time to sleep. We have school tomorrow." His eyes twinkled. An idea popped into his head. "I know now what to do! I'll go the library and find the *book!*" he blurted out, thrilling Argos.

"What book?" Lucy lifted her book.

"I'm not telling!" Eli rubbed his hands together.

Argos glared at his hands. "No healing light. You're just a *Gris*. That book is too powerful for your taking, given your corrupt nature. Once you find it, I will snatch it away."

Harold tapped Eli on the shoulder. He stuck his index fingers on his forehead, prodding him to join him in scaring Lucy. "We need to boot her out," he mouthed.

Eli weighed in for a moment.

"Lucy, what's that behind you?" Harold started, pointing past her, against the wall fronting Eli's bed.

Argos moved back, hitting a stud.

"Nuh-uh," she refused, covering her face with the book.

"N-no. Seriously, you should check it out," Eli persuaded, faking a nervous tone.

Lucy slowly pulled out from her cover, buying his trick. Craning her neck around, she asked with shivering voice, "W-what is it?"

A shadow with horns cast on the wall greeted her. She screamed her lungs out and threw her book in fright.

Frantic footsteps erupted in the hallway.

The doorknob clicked. Stella strode in quickly. She groped for the light switch, dazzling everyone, including

Argos. "What's going on here?" she asked nervously. Her eyes roamed around the room, past the children.

The spinning bird shadows ceased.

Argos gingerly tiptoed toward Eli's headboard to avoid Stella.

Noah appeared. His hair was in disarray and his left cheek bore a sleep tattoo.

Lucy ran to Stella. "They were scaring me!"

Harold made a whooping laugh which disintegrated into an endless, raspy cough.

Noah cleared his throat.

"But Dad, she got scared of her own shadow!" Eli explained.

"No! It was a *bogeyman* with two horns!" Lucy insisted.

The boys let out a chortle they quickly contained after Noah gave them a stern look.

Stella exhaled. "They were just tricking you," she advised, controlling her disappointment. "Like there is no *talking mini-comet* landing in our house," she continued, almost in a whisper.

"Mom heard?" Harold mouthed at Eli.

"Stop pretending you're surprised. You're the tattletale," he mouthed back.

Noah let out a big yawn.

Stella prodded Lucy to go to her own room. She refused.

"But I'm scared to sleep alone. What if there's really a bogeyman?" she insisted.

Noah stooped down to her level. "Fear grows in the dark. If you really think there's a bogeyman, just switch the light on and it will go away," he imparted, stroking her hair. His tired eyes wandered toward the lamp. "See, the lamp is on!"

"Can I sleep in your room just for tonight? Please?" she pleaded with praying hands.

"But Dad just told you there is no bogeyman," Stella reiterated.

"I'm still scared!" she pouted, about to cry.

Noah gave Stella a look of surrender. "Oh, OK. But just for tonight."

Lucy rushed to her book on the floor. "Will you read for me before I sleep?" she then asked Noah, rendering him speechless.

"I will read for you," Stella volunteered, sparing Noah, who shrugged helplessly. "But haven't you heard enough stories for the night?"

"But their stories give me nightmares."

"Then you shouldn't have stayed in their room in the first place. It's your curiosity that made you afraid. What you don't know won't hurt you."

Argos watched Eli crumple his face under the pillow in disagreement.

"Yay! I'm not going to have bad dreams!" Lucy left, rejoicing.

Noah scratched his head while he tailed her. "Pray so you won't have bad dreams," he admonished; his tired voice bounced off the hallway walls.

"Good night, boys." Stella switched off the light.

"Night, Mom," Eli and Harold chorused.

The door clicked.

The bird shadows returned.

Harold watched the ceiling for a minute. He dozed off fast.

Eli took his eyeglasses off and placed it under the lamp. He laid on his back and watched the spinning shadows. He stayed awake.

Argos joined in. Sadness glistened in his eyes. "The lamp and the chandelier are your personal stamps. You missed the *Celebration of Lights*."

The clock ticked aloud.

Eli grumbled silently. He could hear the clock's hand ticking slowly. "Argh! I don't want to feel the time. Please, stop stalling the night," he whispered with praying hands.

The wind blew.

He bolted out of his bed. "You forgot to close the window," he barked at Harold.

Argos pulled his head. For a moment, he thought he was speaking to him.

Harold snored in reply.

Eli reached for the latch. He stopped cranking after noticing a handful of bright lights flickering from a distance. "Fireflies."

Argos turned to the backyard. He stood side by side with him, joining him in his amusement.

A firefly wandered from the group.

Eli straightened up. "*Mini-comet,* tell me what is it you want?"

"The *Chronicles of Light!*" Argos replied.

The lost firefly found its way back.

Argos crumpled his face. "I can't go home without the book. But I don't want to be imprisoned here in Evergreen. I don't want to be like Prince Elijah."

"Of course, you need to go back to your family," Eli said, referring to the firefly.

"My *family*." Argos turned teary-eyed.

Eli noticed the full moon. He observed clusters of rocks on its surface - some bright, some dull. He cranked the latch again, then paused. The fireflies lost in number. He removed his hand from the latch, then made a fist.

"You must gather together so you can emit great light. Learn from the moon," he lectured, pointing to the sky. "Those rocks aren't all bright and big, but clustered together, you are powerful."

"There is indeed strength in numbers," Argos approved.

Eli yawned. "Well, that was quite an entertainment," he said; his voice relaxing and his curled, long eyelashes growing heavy. He closed the window tightly. His bed called for him. He spread his body and pulled the quilt up to his neck.

"See you tomorrow," Argos said thickly. He yawned wide while moving toward Harold's bed. About to lie down on the dusty floor, he remembered Harold's gift of hearing. He leaned against his headboard and whispered inaudible words.

Harold swatted the air as if a fly was buzzing in his ear. "Leave me alone! Of course, I heard you! Stop! I want to sleep!" he shouted, prompting Eli to bolt out of his rest.

"W-who doesn't want to leave you alone?" he asked nervously, his eyes pacing between him and the window he knew he closed tight.

Harold flipped his body away, leaving him wondering in the dark.

Chapter 8:
Mirror, Mirror on the Wall

"Prince Elijah! Prince Elijah!" a male voice frantically called out.

Eli woke up. "Dad?" he asked, looking straight at the door.

The voice called again. His name boomed through the open window.

The curtain blew.

His eyebrows furrowed. "I locked it before I slept!" he grumbled while throwing himself out of the bed. The metal frame of his eyeglasses glinted. "Oh, no! The albino!" he suddenly remembered. He ran to the window and reached his spot in a flash. He cranked his face back to his bed, looking baffled. "Did I just do that?"

Something tickled his left cheek. He whirled about and was greeted by a tree branch. He moved back, surprised how the tree was uprooted from its spot and planted way too close to their house. "And how did you grow in height and width?" he observed. More trees moved. His jaws dropped. "Our garden is now a jungle!"

Colorful flowers sprouted: tulips, peonies, cosmos, anemones, and petunias. He watched in bewilderment as their tiny heads blossomed to the size of a ceiling lamp's mouth. The tender stalks looked sturdy, like pieces of a metal rod. As each shot up about seven feet high, the heads started glowing. They opened and closed, like hands, and spurted colorful sparkles. He licked the air by reflex. "Caramel," he said, surprised by his action.

The neon flower heads glowed brighter and brighter. The air tasted sweeter and sweeter. In the sky, rainbows appeared. Sweet music played.

"But there's no rain," he pointed out. "And where is this music coming from?"

An overdose of oxygen blew his way. The vinyl sidings rattled.

He touched his cheeks. It felt warm. "It's just a dream, right? But how come it feels so real?" he said, awed.

His name floated back.

Frantic footsteps emerged.

He gasped. "He's running toward me!" The grasses scrunched. "W-what is your business with me? And who are you running from?" he asked in a row.

A dark mist descended. It cloaked the garden. The neon lightposts wilted. The mist took form as a silhouete of a towering male figure seemingly wearing a long cape. He held a huge book in his right hand, which he used like a sword, stabbing everything with life: the trees, flowers, moon, and stars. Dreadful eeriness filled the air. The rainbows vanished. The music went silent. Before the moon died, it cast light over the man's face.

"Dad?" he asked.

The silhouette overheard. He flipped the cape; he realized were wings, like a raven's. When he took off and steered toward his room, he nervously moved away. "H-how can you fly?"

Darkness seeped in. He sought the lamp's light, but its bulb started flickering. Up in the ceiling, the spinning bird shadows fell off their orbits.

A strong gust of wind blew his way – the silhouette was flying outside his window. He unfurled his fingers and from his long claws came out dark vapors. It crawled on the walls, ceiling, and floor, like mold. The room turned into a black hole.

The spinning lamp stopped.

Everything vanished, including Harold. He shrunk on his feet, clutching his chest, pinned down by the lingering darkness he realized weighed heavy on his spirit. From the corner of his eyes, he noticed the silhouette basking at the swirling darkness he created.

"Fear grows in the dark. If you really think there's a bogeyman, just switch the light on and it will go away," he declared, surprised he memorized Noah's advice to Lucy. He glanced back at the silhouette. "You can't fool me. Dad won't let me grope in the dark! Impostor! Remove your mask!" he barked while starting for the switch near the door. He tried to feel it, but he couldn't find it. "You flushed it out!"

The silhouette entered his room. He spread his raven wings, which he mentally calculated covered three meters breadth for each wing. In his wrap was the huge black book. A torn page stuck out. He looked on closely and noticed he was murmuring inaudible words, like a spell.

"Prince Elijah! Help me! Help me, Eli" The voice whimpered.

Eli squirmed. "H-how can I help you? You're in the woods. The distance…"

The silhouette cackled.

"Why are you happy he's hurting?" he asked, incensed by his callousness.

Goosebumps struck. His heart burned. His eyes and skin too. He looked at his hands and was shocked to see himself rolling his hands over his hollow chest as if kneading a dough. A foam of light appeared on each palm. "Whoa! Where did this come from?" he asked, surprised yet liking it.

The light gained mass, about the size of a football. The darkened room began to brighten up. The walls and ceiling appeared anew. Harold popped back on his bed. The lamp played like a turntable. The bird shadows returned to their orbit. The grim vibe dissipated.

Eli turned to the silhouette, who, to his surprise, was in a quandary trying to escape, scorched by the room's light. "Get out of my room!" he shouted, swinging the ball of light in his hands.

The ball of light sizzled. He ran to the window and saw it hit the silhouette. He turned into a dark mist, while the huge black book went up in flames. Embers fizzled out. The ball of light blazed away, travelling quite a distance. It struck a tree, causing it to glow brightly.

"That far?"

The voice gasped as if resuscitated back to life.

Eli listened on his feet. The voice left. He smiled, feeling heroic. About to go back to his bed, his right foot stubbed into something—a white, compact mirror with tiny, cut diamonds on its rim. His eyes grew as big as saucers. He excitedly stooped down to pick it up. The diamond's glow touched his skin. He felt refreshed like he just woke up from a long, deep sleep.

"Time to wake up," he told himself. "But when I do, I want to see you in my grasp still."

The moment the words escaped his lips, the mirror escaped his clutch and floated in the air. His jaws dropped. He checked his feet. He stayed grounded as did everything else in the room. The mirror clamped itself against the wall near his headboard. It grew in size, similar to an oval-shaped door.

"Mirror, mirror on the wall," he whispered, edging his way in.

The clock stopped ticking.

Eli noticed everything stayed stationary: the blowing curtain, the spinning bird shadows, and the turning lamp. On the floor, something shimmered. "Water?" He quickly touched his crotch, thinking he peed unaware. He moved away from it, feeling embarrassed. It followed him. "My shadow?"

Something moved on the mirror. He turned toward it. In quick intervals, his reflection transformed into a middle-aged, glowing angel with blurred face dressed in golden armour, holding a golden sword, then to a familiar old man wearing a charcoal suit, and lastly, back to his usual self. From the corner of his eye, in the midst of his nervous marveling, he saw the windowsill glowing. Only then did he realize the whizzing sound, sort of a firework, was heading toward his room.

A bright light exploded.

The room was illuminated. The walls and ceiling moved acres away, the light expanding its size. The walls shimmered like a waterfall, prompting him to check his shadow. He gasped. He looked like he was floating in the air! The light covered the entire floor! He turned to Harold. He slept like a baby; his bed in the middle of what seemed like a sea of white fair clouds.

The wind blew. He snorted. It smelled minty.

About to check the window, his gaze flitted toward the mirror. It turned into a giant emerald. "The garden is back!" he beamed, about to run toward it. He froze, feeling conflicted. “But the garden is that way,” he said, panning his face toward the window.

The minty scent reeked.

He inched toward the mirror and took a peek. He saw herbal plants, some of them he named: “Burdock, aloe vera, Neem…”

The clock ticked again.

His eyes darted to the clock. The bright light shrank, sucked in by the absent vaccum room he thought for a moment was the window. “Off to the moon,” he laughed.

The room turned back to its original size. The walls turned ordinary again.

The light gathered into a hill behind him. He squirmed, touched by its minty radiance. His eyes widened seeing a shadow of a towering, sparkly figure on the floor.

The angel in the mirror! He stepped out! He wanted to scream, but he couldn’t find his voice.

Goosebumps struck. The minty scent rubbed his nose. Shortly, he found himself floating, carried by a pair of strong hands.

He dozed off.

Chapter 9:
Pass the Word!

The rooster crowed.

Eli woke up, kicked in the face by the morning sun. He quickly flipped to his left, avoiding the glaring window, only to see Harold standing in the doorway, dressed for school.

"Beat you!" he shouted before rushing down the stairs.

"No!" Eli threw himself out of the bed and hit the ceiling, at least that was what it felt in his head. "Argh!" he cried, beset with a migraine. He massaged his temples. "He's the hero again," he fretted, sinking in self-pity. His eyes suddenly lighted up. A snigger managed to etch its way into his grimace. "Last night, in my dream, I was a hero!" He snapped his fingers twice, then unfurled his palms quickly after, as if playing rock-paper-scissor by himself. "No light?" He tried again, producing none. He then rubbed his palms together, causing some warmth, but mainly out of friction. He paused, staring blankly into the air, processing his dream. He then glared at his palms, observing the discreet lines. "Could it be there's more to just being me?"

The clock ticked.

"Seven o'clock!" He panicked. He bolted out of his bed and went straight to the closet. He opened it but paused as he was about to scroll over the pile of neatly, folded clothes. He glanced back to his bed, mentally calculating the time it took him to reach his spot. His eyes ran to the window. "I'm becoming like Lucy, addicted to fairy tales," he said, rolling his eyes.

The daylight clapped through the window. His eyes drifted nervously. "The albino! He's the reason of this craziness. Where did he get his super shoes?" he rambled, feeling frustrated. "I'm going to the library. That's my ground zero. I have to put an end to this fantasy!" His fingers landed on a collared, green long-sleeve shirt, and jersey pants. He grabbed them and stormed into the bathroom in the hallway, and took his shower.

Five minute passed. He showed up, dressed. His wet hair dripped on his collar. He grabbed his eyeglasses on the bedside table, then rushed downstairs. While treading the stairs, he feared Harold took his chair in his absence. The moment he landed on the main floor, he ran to the dining room. He found him in his usual spot, eating a bowl of cereals. His collared, red shirt was tucked in flat; his hair slicked back. He sighed, relieved he didn't take his spot, but his going ahead of him left a bad taste in his mouth. Heading for his chair, he felt Lucy's questioning eyes on him.

"You're late," she pointed out.

"I, uh, slept in," he explained, briefly glancing her way.

"Did you really? Why not check the mirror and look at your face?" Lucy stuck her right thumb behind her.

Eli froze on his feet. He turned to the mirror like a robot, the remote control on Lucy's hand. He gasped. Her crown was glowing! His nostrils flared while sifting the morning air, searching for anything minty. He stopped looking when her baffled eyes met his. Embarrassed, he sat down. The morning light bounced against the mirror from the huge bay window in the living room. About to lower his eyes, he caught sight of the pictures on display on top of the sideboard. He combed the pictures from his spot and saw the picture of his father. "That wasn't him. Dad is not evil," he mused softly, recalling his dream. About to sit down, he took a second look and saw his grandfather's solo picture where he wore his charcoal suit. "What were you doing in my dream, Grandpa?"

Lucy giggled. "LOL! You are so beside yourself. I told you it will *eat* you up," she jeered. "Just don't *burn* us, okay," she said, her giggles fading.

"B-burn?" Eli lifted his palms.

Harold rubbed his hands.

"W-what are you doing?"

"Pinch or punch?" Harold offered.

Eli's cheeks blushed. He reached for the cereal box and the pitcher of milk in the middle of the table, pretending he heard none. His ears burned while listening to Harold telling Lucy how he begged for it last night. Then he remembered his outburst. *You spoke with the albino!* His face soured with the spoonful of cereals suspended near his opened lips. He wanted to ask him, but he refrained. "I'm playing it smart this time. He will confess! He's a talking machine! I must dethrone him. I can't be a hero and villain at the same time. That's absurd!" he thought aloud.

Something bright flashed through the kitchen window, hitting the spoon in his hand. His eyes gleamed. He ran to the living room, saddled his backpack resting near the foot of the stairs, then rushed to open the front door. He overheard Lucy complaining about him making everything a race.

Rays of light knocked in through the door slits. He took a deep breath while cranking the doorknob. Opening the door, the morning light bathed him. The spring air breezed in, filling his chest with the aroma of their garden in the backyard.

"It's a gooooood morning!" Harold shouted from behind.

Eli watched him walk him past, strutting with a swagger. He looked a bit slender, courtesy of the big, red stripes on his shirt. But scrolling down to his tight, jersey pants, he sneered with contempt. His legs looked like sausages. *You are fat and slow! If that albino shows up again, I will outrace you!*

The sunlight kicked his face, stopping his poor appraisal of Harold. He turned to the bright and cloudless sky; his right hand over his forehead. He smiled while imagining the huge windows in the school library drawing in the light, then illuminating all the books on the shelves.

Carpe diem, he thought aloud with a guaranteed smile, promising to get his vindication before the day ends.

"Why are you smiling?" Lucy materialized on his right.

Eli flinched. "Why don't you mind your own business," he barked, deeply worried how his day would pan out if she kept on checking him.

Stella appeared on his left. He felt cornered, afraid she'd join Lucy in her interrogation. But when she pointed to the crocus and perennials in the garden, he sighed in relief. "The flowers always tell me something," she announced, sniffing.

"And what could be it?" Lucy wondered.

Eli quickly stayed out of her line of sight, glad she set aside her survey on him.

"*Hope.*"

"Hope?"

Stella nodded. "Yes, flowers speak hope," she explained, wrapping her arms around her body, feeling the bite of the cool morning wind.

Lucy took a deep breath. "I'll pick some for you later, after school," she promised, looking forward. She checked the time on her pink, analog wristwatch. "It's almost seven thirty! We'll be late if we don't start running now!" she told Harold and Eli.

Harold went ahead. "Chill. We won't be late," he assured, smiling smugly. "Girl, you read time before you could read books!"

"Oh," she quipped, surprised by his unusual flattery. "Looks like someone woke up feeling good today. What's with you?"

"He has *secrets!*" Eli talked out his suspicion right off the bat.

Lucy's face beamed. "I'm intrigued."

Harold wiggled his right foot in the air. "It's tight!"

"Then you will not kick up a storm on the way to school," Eli held, intent at raining on his parade.

"Not today!" Harold lifted his double chin.

"It's going to be a race then," he guaranteed.

Harold scoffed. "That's why I tied my shoes tight!" he fired back, throwing a soft nudge on his elbow.

"Game on!" Eli turned around fast, upset his challenge went out flat. He watched him walk away spilling with energy. He thought, "Obviously, he had a good sleep. Plus, he struck a conversation with my albino! No wonder he is feeling really good. He has his aces up."

Lucy checked the port. It was empty. "Dad went out early," she mused, pouting. "I wish he gave us a ride."

"Not today," Stella answered. "By the way, are all of your books inside your bags?" she remembered to ask, prompting everyone to halt.

"We left our books in the lockers," Harold replied fast and in a loud voice, besting his

siblings who gawked at his competition. "It's heavy on the back," he explained matter-of-factly, reducing Eli to an adamant nod.

Stella continued, "How about your water bottles?"

Lucy quickly checked the side pocket of her bag. "Why is my water bottle clear? I want the pink one!" she fretted.

Eli checked his bag's side pocket too. It contained the same clear, water bottle. "Thanks, Mom!" he told her, realizing she secretly slipped in the water bottle while Lucy stalled him on the porch.

"Sneaky me," she said, flashing a candid smile.

Lucy went on complaining. "I want the pink one! This clear bottle is so plain and big!"

"Quit it, *Your Highness,*" Harold taunted. "Mom gave me the biggie too," he said, swaying his bag to show his bottle.

"Biggie fits you," she fired back.

"At least we have spare," Eli exclaimed half-heartedly.

"Like we need it," Harold opposed, rolling his eyes. "We have drinking fountains in school. We can always refill."

"Some kids spit on it you know."

"Euw! Gross!" Lucy shrieked.

"You all go now. It's going to be a long walk." Stella absently clutched her chest. Her eyes wandered toward Lucy's flat shoes.

"Gotta go, Mom!" Lucy motioned to her brothers.

"See you later, Mom!" Harold shouted, waiving his both hands in the air. He quickly tucked in his slightly-loosened shirt. "I don't want to lose my style," he told Lucy.

"Nobody likes you," she said, earning a growl from him.

Eli gave Stella a timid wave. When she started checking the dark circles under his eyes, he turned around fast and sped up, going ahead of his siblings. After covering enough space, he cranked his head around to check on her. She remained on her feet, surprisingly, eyeing the trees. Shortly, she was running toward them. His eyebrows furrowed. "That's weird."

"Stop touching my hair! I don't want to go back inside the house to check myself in the mirror!" Lucy yelled, grabbing his attention.

Harold sniggered. "You're such a doll! Pink pigtails, pink dress, and pink cardigan!" he shouted—his voice bounced against the trees lining up the driveway.

"I'm a princess, *Dumbo!*" Lucy pulled away.

Eli shrugged, not wanting to meddle. The trees cleared out. Reverend Goodfellow's shiny black coupe's tail greeted him. His feet lost steam. His eyes wandered to his door. He thought of knocking, but judging by the car's position, he doubted its involvement from last night. He moved on, shaking his head. He imagined the library. He rubbed his fingers, eager to turn pages. When he caught up with Lucy, he found her standing pointedly in front of the neighbor's rusty mailbox, next to Reverend Goodfellow's house.

"S-p-e-a-r-s," she read softly, patiently uttering each letter's sound. "Spears!"

"Wow! You're getting there!"

"I want to read on my own soon!"

"So, it means, we're not going to see each other in the library later," he said, crossing his fingers.

Lucy sneered. "Of course not! The usual!" she said, nodding her head. Her pigtails bounced against her shoulders.

Harold asked, "Why are you two going on a date?"

"We're reading buddies! Don't you know?" Lucy smirked.

"Cut the smirk, will you? Don't you sour my day! I woke up feeling great today!"

"But how come you don't know?" she fired back, adding, "We're siblings! We should know everything about each other. No *secrets!*"

Eli's pace turned ponderous. "Lucy's right! Harold has been throwing dust in my eyes since last night! It's time for him to blow the whistle!" he thought while inching his way toward him. About to open his lips, eager to interrogate, a truck hustled from the south. He flinched, startled by the noise.

"You want to hitch?" Harold probed. "Wrong way. That truck is going to the marketplace, where the *bogeyman* lives," he continued, making a spooky face.

"The albino is the bogeyman," he whispered, considering the possibility. "But how about the angel in my dream?"

"A thief is no angel!" Harold walked away.

Eli chased him, not wanting to be on his tail. Reaching his spot, he found him kicking a tiny stone over and over.

"I'm just amusing myself so I don't feel this long walk to school," he excused.

Eli smiled naughtily.

"Why are you smiling?"

"If only that stone will follow you," he said, giving the stone a meaningful glance.

"What do you mean?"

"Imagine a stone chasing you, you'll run your butt off to school! For sure you'll win the race. That will be another *history* in the making!" Eli laughed in sarcastic cuts.

Harold smirked. "I wish, but I don't have *fancy imagination* like yours," he said, wiping away the smug grin off his face.

Eli stopped laughing. "So, you didn't…"

"You're weird! For the record!" Harold gave him a whimsical gaze.

"Oh well," was all he said.

The chimneys along the street blew.

Eli watched Harold slow down. He started sniffing hard. He overheard him say, "I wish our dinner tonight will be a feast." He rolled his eyes.

"Like Christmas balls," Lucy cut in.

Eli panned to her. She was gliding her fingers against the colorful flowers on the side road. "You're both daydreaming," he rebuked, only to feel guilty. "I started this chain of fantasy."

They reached the final turn. Simultaneously, they stopped in front of the corner house with its bare front yard, and were pulled in by the squeaky rocking chair swaying doleful, as usual.

"Good morning, *Mrs. Linda*." Lucy greeted.

Mrs. Linda stayed quiet.

Harold made a face-palm. "Stop being nice and friendly!"

Lucy frowned. "I can't help myself. Besides, *manners*," she stressed with a hand gesture.

"Banner – Manner. That rhymes. That's us. It doesn't work for her."

The wind blew softly.

Lucy sniffed. "I smell something," she said, looking for its origin.

Eli turned to her, almost frenetic. "What are you smelling?" he asked, hoping she'd say it smelled minty. His eyes darted back to the bushes on the side of the house, looking for any spark behind the chinks.

"Something fragrant," she said, still snorting.

"An explosion of fragrance is either a garden or a funeral," Harold stated matter-of-factly. "And since she has no garden –"

Lucy shoved him. "You are sooo dark!"

Eli pressed his face forward and took a deep inhale. "She's wearing a perfume! What gives?" he shouted, unable to control his surprise.

Lucy pushed her face closer to the porch, flagrantly snooping. "Where is she going?"

Eli moved closer to the porch. He noticed she tied her long, salt and pepper hair in a chignon for the first time. She wore brand-new, flat shoes too. The price tags were still attached. Her knee-high yellowish silky dress looked sunny, but it accentuated her fragile frame. When his eyes landed on the white cane, which she had clearly wiped clean, sitting on her lap, he ended his probing. "She's not going anywhere."

"Maybe she's waiting for someone," Harold guessed.

"Or something. Her mail." Lucy glanced at the rustic, blank mailbox erected on a piece of wood on her lawn.

Harold gazed at Mrs. Linda's clouded hazel eyes and went on coldly, "I wonder how she could read if she's..."

"Hush. She's not deaf," Eli rebuked, nudging him hard on the elbow which he parried easily.

"She made effort today. She must be *in-love.*" Lucy blinked wistfully.

Harold scoffed. "She's a widow. You don't suppose."

"Oh no! Erase that!" Lucy rubbed her forehead with her clenched fist. "Why did I even come up with that?" Pondering, her eyes twinkled. "Aha! She's going to a party!" she shared, prompting her brothers to laugh. "No? Not a good idea?"

"If she's going to a party, then she should be happy!" Harold pointed his right hand toward Mrs. Linda, impassioned. "She wore her best, but she still looks sad," he declared, taking note of the wrinkles around her eyes and lips. "Dad said she's just a few years ahead of him, but she looks like she's his aunt."

"Well, she's ready to go," Eli said.

"But you said she's not going anywhere!" Lucy countered.

"We don't know that. Maybe, when we reach school, her chariot will arrive," he said, tickling her fantasy which he regretted immediately.

"She's a *princess* too!" Lucy clapped her hands over her chest in delight. "Wow. We're the same!"

Harold shushed her. "I don't like this *princess* talk."

Eli looked past Mrs. Linda and noticed the frosted wall lanterns flanking the front door were still turned on. "It's already morning. What a waste of electricity!" he said, shaking his head.

"Duh! She's well-off," Harold claimed, adding, "She can afford to waste electricity, and buy costly silk dresses and expensive perfumes."

"But she doesn't see how blessed she is." Eli's voice trailed off. He scanned her and was disheartened. She looked like a zombie with her pale skin, frail frame, sitting lifeless. "L-let's go," he told Harold and Lucy. "We'll be late."

A burst of wind blew toward her porch. Her hunched spine suddenly straightened up, pulled by an invisible cord he felt was in his hand. She leaned forward, prompting him to move back. When her depleted chest took a sharp inhale, he looked on interestedly. She was resuscitated! Her weary, cloudy eyes turned vibrant and her pale cheeks blushed. When her eyes met his, he gasped in shock.

"You're a Banner." Her voice sounded like it was hauled from the depths.

"Y-yes," he replied, surprised to see her engaging for the first time.

"What's your name?"

"Eli."

"Eli," she repeated, tasting his name in her buds. "Your name rings a bell."

Eli shrugged taciturnly. "Well, I was named after my grandfather – the late *reverend*," he relayed, hoping she'd recognize it. "A-anyways, I'm really sorry for our nonsense rambling," he apologized, about to leave.

"Do me a favour," she interrupted.

"S-sure!" Eli awkwardly climbed the first step of the porch, assuming she needed help to go back inside the house.

"Tell *him* that I've been waiting," she begged, sounding so lost and full of longing.

"Tell *who?*"

Harold tapped Eli on the shoulder. "What are you doing? You shooed us away so you can stay behind? What's your business with her?" he ranted, looking annoyed.

"She spoke!" he nervously shared.

The rocking chair swayed doleful again. Mrs. Linda slipped back to her usual self.

"Just so you know, you keep on eating your own words!" Harold accused, dragging his heavy feet away.

Eli tailed him, looking confused.

Lucy angrily showed him her watch.

"She asked me to carry a *message* for her!" he shared, intriguing her.

"What *message?*"

"She told me to tell *him* that she's been waiting," he revealed with crumpled face.

"Him who?" Harold's interest was stirred, although just in passing.

"Must be the mailman," Eli guessed. He tossed his head away, wanting to bury the subject right away.

Chapter 10: A Flock of Crows is Called a Murder

Eli caught a silhouette watching them from the second-floor window of Mrs. Linda's house. The white, vinyl blinds shook. His eyes narrowed. "Why does she have to ask me when her son is upstairs?" he asked, trying in vain to drain the irritation from his voice.

Lucy waived her right hand, but Harold restrained her quickly. She glanced back at the window and asked, "Why doesn't he go to school?"

"He's home-schooled!" Eli explained irritably.

"Obviously, you're not friends," she replied, thrown off by his tone. "What's his name?"

"Lior."

"So, you know his name," she said.

Eli sneered. "FYI, we're not friends," he clarified, adding, "Besides, he hardly speaks to anyone."

Lucy smirked. "What a snub!" she blasted, glancing at the window for the last time.

Harold glared briefly at the window before looking away. "When a need arises he'll look for a friend, that's for sure," he guaranteed, lifting his double chin.

The number of houses dwindled. The dusty main road split, the right lane heading toward the woods.

Eli stopped walking. On the other side of the trees, the dense trees waved "Hi."

Prince Elijah! Help me!

The voice in his dream echoed in his mind repeatedly, like an alarm clock.

His hands rose to his chest by reflex. "Why do I get this feeling that night is just about to happen?" he wondered, looking steadfast at the woods.

A breeze blew in.

"It was just a dream," he said, dropping his hands. He turned to his left, opting to take the main road, but he felt a strong pull to the right, toward the woods.

"Make up your mind," Lucy hollered from behind. "This way or that way?" she asked with her arms straddled out in both directions.

A black coupe stopped in front of them.

"Reverend Goodfellow!" she shouted.

Reverend Goodfellow rolled down his side mirror. "Good morning, Princess Lucy!" he greeted candidly. "My goodness! You look so much like your mom! Two peas in a pod!"

Lucy tried hard not to gaze at the huge black mole under his right eye—the mother of all moles—on his ancient face. "I like the color of your suit. It matches your mo…" she paused, biting her lower lip.

"I'm sorry I didn't hear you," Reverend Goodfellow apologized. He turned off the engine and said, "Now that's better. So, what did you say again?" he asked Lucy.

"I, um… I said, that's what I'm told by everybody. I do look like Mom," she replied, tongue-in-cheek. "And yes, your suit looks familiar," she added with a fake smile.

Reverend Goodfellow beamed. "Of course. Your late grandfather wore the same. It's our, well, uniform in the church," he answered, feeling proud. "Do you want a ride?" he offered, turning his face toward Harold and Eli.

Harold and Lucy nodded their heads fast like bobbleheads.

Eli refused.

Harold and Lucy grumbled in protest.

Eli shot them a stern look that they refused to understand. "Reverend Goodfellow has better things to do than to give us a lift. We don't want to be a bother and make him scramble for his missed time."

Reverend Goodfellow tapped his fingers against the steering wheel. His antiqued silver wristwatch and diamond ring briefly took Eli's eyes. "Well, I do have a meeting that will commence in a few minutes," he admitted. "Although I do believe they will forgive me for coming in late."

"You should go ahead," Eli replied, saying the words in one giant breath. "It's not nice to make people wait."

Harold sighed. "We can manage."

Lucy hummed lethargically.

"We won't keep you hanging now, sir," Eli continued, gripping his backpack strap tighter.

Reverend Goodfellow understood his gesture. About to start the engine, he looked at Eli's face steadily as if memorizing every bit of it. His receding hairline began stretching out like he remembered something amazing. But in a flick of a finger, his smiling eyes turned sentimental. "Y-you remind me of your grandfather," he said, sounding contrite. "He was a good man. A good friend. The best minister this town ever had," he continued with the corners of his mouth pointing down.

Eli nodded timidly. "You told me about that. Many times, in fact."

Reverend Goodfellow smiled bitterly. "You also got his name." He looked past him and stared blankly at the woods.

"Have a good day," Harold interrupted.

"Oh!" Reverend Goodfellow quipped, somehow awakened. "Harold! Harold!" he repeated. "I almost forgot! Before I start running, I have something here for you," he said, twisting his arched body to the passenger side.

Eli peeked. He saw him reach out for a brown box wrapped with a red ribbon, tucked under a thick, dog-eared, black-leather Bible just like theirs. He zeroed in on the bible. His wary eyes lit up. "I'm going to find that book that will give me vindication. You go now, Reverend. I have a mission to fulfill," he thought, itching to bolt away. Suddenly, he remembered the huge black book the silhouette possessed. He shook his head. "Not that book! That book is evil!"

Reverend Goodfellow wiggled the brown box in the air before handing it to Harold. "Belated happy birthday!" he sang, sounding upbeat.

"Wow! Thank you!" Harold unwrapped it quickly. He pulled out a wooden slingshot. "Wow! I'm leveling up! No more just watching bird shadows! This time it's for real!" he declared, making a happy dance after; his flab folding. He then aimed his slingshot against the sky and made popping sounds.

Eli looked on enviously.

"That," Reverend Goodfellow said, pointing to his gift, "was my favorite pastime when I was your age! Just be careful. Handle it with caution. It can also be a weapon," he admonished, slipping back into his usual pondering quickly after.

"Weapon? But this is just wood." Harold scratched his head.

Reverend Goodfellow clicked his tongue. "Ah, you'd be surprised, *good things come in small packages!*" he averred, sighing after. "Well, I must keep going now. But please stay away from the woods. Just use the main road. It's safer," he continued, earning quizzical gazes from them. "I know you've heard me say it before, but it doesn't hurt to be reminded over and over, just so we don't forget," he instructed, tapping his right index finger on his temple. The engine revved up. He stepped on the gas and drove away.

Lucy waited for the coupe to vanish from her sight. When all she could see was the dust it left behind, she grumbled to Eli. "You're a killjoy!"

Eli crossed the street. "I don't want to inconvenience him. He has a meeting. You heard him yourself," he explained. "Besides, there's a shortcut to the school playground through the woods. That's going to save us at least five minutes."

"Reverend Goodfellow said not to go this way," Harold reminded Eli, feeling guilty. "Look, he just gave me a gift. I don't want to repay his kindness with disobedience."

"Yeah!" Lucy agreed. "That's not good. Reverend Goodfellow is like a grandfather to us!"

Eli walked on, ignoring their valid excuses.

The trees rustled as if welcoming him.

The voice returned.

"Here I am," he mumbled softly.

Daylight shone like a helicopter with a floodlight beam highlighting the path ahead. He followed it and entered a shade. Sunlight trickled through the chinks. He secretly checked each tree while snorting hard. "Show yourself, *albino.* Whoever you are," he whispered.

"Stop making conversation with yourself!" Lucy rebuked. "And chop-chop! We'll be late if you don't speed up," she continued, showing him her watch.

Harold giggled. "He's Eli–*fied!*"

"Eli–*fied?*" she repeated. "What does that mean?"

"Eli–*fied!*" Harold made a stoic face and started walking like a zombie.

Lucy burst into laughter. "LOL! I suddenly remembered Mrs. Linda," she quipped, covering her mouth quickly after. "I'm sorry. That was rude."

"I know, right! Mrs. Linda was really stoned!" Harold laughed his head off.

Eli frowned. "Genius," he praised. "Stop being being Harold-*ish,*" he fired back, causing his flood of giggles to cease.

"Wait, what's 'Harold-*ish*' this time?" Lucy tried hard to suppress her giggles. "It sounds like it has something to do with food."

"Being goofy, dissing, like he always does," he described, blowing his cheeks to make them plump.

Harold blushed. "Not funny!"

"Wait! What about me? Give me a name too!" she demanded.

Harold blinked his eyes naughtily. He tapped his double chin and mused. "Lucy. Hmm. What new name should I give you? How about Lucy – *fer?*"

Eli almost choked at this suggestion.

"Lucy-*fer*? Sounds familiar." Lucy's eyes blinked whimsically.

"It's the devil's name! Idiot!" Eli enlightened.

Lucy's smile turned to a growl. She pushed Harold hard, intent on putting him down on the ground, but his weight kept him upright. "You're so dark! I'm no she-devil! Stop being Harold-*ish, Dumbo!*"

Harold sneered. "You asked for it, *Crying Princess!*"

"As I was saying before Harold made up a twisted vocabulary of names," she said, panning to Eli. "You were talking to yourself! You were sniffing while walking! You are weird!"

"Eli was out!" Harold sputtered.

"My guess is you were looking for your *talking mini-comet!*" she continued.

Eli flinched. "N-no. I wasn't," he stammered. "I just thought..." he paused, strangling his thoughts in the air, leaving them hanging in suspense.

"If only I could read your mind." Lucy sighed in surrender.

Harold gave him a stink-eye.

"W-what?" Eli returned his odd stare.

Lucy exhaled in exasperation. "You're here, but you're *not* here," she noted, tapping her right temple.

Harold scoffed. "S-p-a-c-y," he spelled out loud. "What's the *word?*" he then asked Lucy abruptly, catching her off guard. "Ticktock, ticktock," he chimed while waiting for her answer; his head swaying like a pendulum.

"Argh! You are making me nervous!" Lucy hyperventilated. "How can I spell it out properly when…"

"I didn't sleep well last night," Eli cut in, breaking off their game.

Lucy's left eyebrow shot up. She then crossed her arms over her chest. "You already confessed to that. The real issue is what kept you up? Obviously, you don't want to share it with us. It is *you* with secrets, not Harold!" she blasted, throwing off Harold.

"So, you were thinking ill about me, huh!" he said, squinting his puppy eyes.

"It ate you up, like I said!" she continued, wiggling her right index finger. She pushed Harold on the left shoulder. "If you didn't scare me last night, we could have talked it out properly! Look at him!" she blamed, feeling angry and concerned at the same time.

"Why is it on me suddenly?" Harold protested. "I wasn't the one lying!"

"Right! Liar, liar! Your eyes on fire!" she sang, pointing her finger at Eli's eyes.

Eli shoved her hand away. "Well, even if I tell the truth, you won't believe me anyways!" He lowered his face to hide his red cheeks. "I will find that book. This shaming ends today," he promised through clenched teeth.

"You were like a crossing guard a while ago," Harold told Lucy as they walked ahead together. "Make up your mind. This way or that way?" he mimicked with arms straddled out, causing her to giggle.

Eli tagged along. He felt left out. He walked slowly, sinking in self-pity when he felt a

presence lurking over his shoulders. "The abino!" he thought aloud. He quickly whirled around, but the trail was empty.

Suddenly, a flock of crows snuck up from somewhere and swept around his head. He took off his bag and swatted them away, hitting a bird. From the bird's claw, he noticed white sparkles that were released, sort of a beach dust. The wind took it away. The rest of the birds attacked Harold and Lucy. Harold scrambled for his slingshot, while Eli picked up a stick he found on the side road. He rushed in, swinging the stick like a sword.

The flock retreated to a nearby tree.

"H-have you heard it said a flock of crows is called a *murder?*" Eli shared nervously while pointing the stick against the birds.

Chapter 11:
The Blood Stone

Lucy scooted behind Eli. "They're not going to kill us, right? I mean, they're just birds. Birds don't hurt humans," she hollered nervously.

The birds cawed calmly.

Harold cupped his ears. "They're so loud!" he complained.

"Too loud?" Eli looked on, baffled by his discomfort.

"Maybe they're hungry." Lucy counted the birds. "One, two… five hungry crows."

"Ahhhhh! Enough of your noise!" Harold grumbled. He picked up a stone and placed it on his slingshot, seething as he pulled the rubber. In one flick, he released the stone, hitting a bird on its head. The crows scrambled away. "Ha! Now you got what you're looking for! Shoo! Shoo!" he shouted, his slingshot up in the air.

Eli looked on puzzled. "Whoa! You're an *accidental Jedi!*" he praised, pointing his stick to his slingshot.

"Beginner's luck," he replied in the same breath of confusion.

Lucy steered back to their supposed route. "Come now! Chop-chop! We'll be late," she advised, prompting them to follow her lead.

Harold stood his ground. "But those crows are a threat!" He crumpled his face hearing their flapping wings whirring against his ears. He turned around and saw them flying on the horizon—five black dots, seemingly chased away.

Eli threw his stick away. "They're just birds," he replied, walking away. "It's too early for you to do your bird-watching."

The school bell rang.

"No!" Eli galloped away.

"Wait for me!" Lucy followed.

Harold lingered. "Let me just grab a stone," he said while searching the ground. His eyes, like saucers, found a spiky, muddy stone. "This will surely hurt," he said, smiling mischievously. He rolled it around his fingers and was cut by its spike. "Ouch!" he cried, dropping the stone. A pinch of his blood dripped over its surface.

"Harold!" Lucy called out.

Harold panned his face toward her. "Coming now!" he said, sucking his finger.

The rock started shaking. A small puddle of blood bubbled underneath. The stone shattered, shedding shards of rubies. It trailed Harold's heels as if having a mind of its own. "Ouch!" he cried, halting. "Wait up! There's a pebble in my shoe!"

Eli and Lucy stopped dead in their tracks.

"Now, we are late," he grumbled.

"Harold's fault," she blamed.

"Yours too," he was quick to emphasize. "If you didn't chat with the reverend…"

Lucy blew raspberries. "You had your share too. You eyeballed Mrs. Linda," she reminded, tapping her right index on her temple. "We ALL contributed to this problem," she stressed with hand gestures.

Eli looked away, pretending he heard none. "Anyways, we still have a five-minute grace period. They'll let us in without late slip if we beat it," he claimed, crossing his fingers.

"That grace period will be gone soon," she replied, doubting Harold's pace. "He's the one always left behind!"

"Hush, Lucy. He saved us from the birds," he whispered while making a spooky face.

Lucy giggled softly. Suddenly, her face turned thoughtful.

Eli watched her eyes train on something. He followed her as she walked toward a row of blue flowers lining the diverging bushy, narrow alley that he just noticed for the first time. "Not now, please," he begged while checking the alley he estimated was newly created. "What the…?" he started to say, noticing freshly-cut bushes sprawled on the ground.

"Harold is still out there," she said, disrupting his survey. "I'll be over before he's even done." She knelt and smelled the flowers. "Wow! Look at you! Where have you been hiding all this time? Why didn't I see your beauty before?" she exclaimed with a lilt.

"That's because we never looked this way," he replied warily while glancing at the alley.

Stems snapped.

"FYI, this isn't the right time," he lectured, shaking his head in dismay.

"Please, Eli. Stop being a killjoy," she requested, smelling her harvest in one giant breath. "These are for Mom. She'll love them for sure." She paused, recalling their chat earlier. "Hope," she smiled. Turning to Eli, she showed him a bunch. "Do you know these flowers?"

Eli deadpanned. He watched Harold in a quandary over his left shoe. "And I thought it was tight! What a fail!" he huffed, throwing his hands in the air.

"It's *forget-me-not,*" she said.

"Forget-me-not, alright," Eli repeated languidly.

Lucy collected more flowers, grabbing her chance while Eli's attention was on Harold.

"Stop it, Lucy," he warned. "Even if my eyes aren't on you, I know what you're doing."

"But they smell so good!" she replied, smelling her bunch again.

The wind blew. Eli touched his nape, bitten by the familiar, minty touch. His nostrils flared. The path was suddenly scented by the smell of Vicks! He snorted hard while he searched for its source.

Lucy heard him sniffing. She grinned, thinking he was finally participating in her delight.

Eli's jaws dropped when a spark lighted up from the diverging alley. It grew bigger and faster, skipping the length. It swooshed past Lucy, throwing bright flares but not scorching the bushes. In a split second, the bright light descended on him. He covered his eyes, dazzled.

"Eli! Where is the book?!" Argos kept on asking.

Eli's face blanched, recognizing his voice. "W-what book are you talking about?" he retorted; his heart doing a rat-a-tat. He watched the grasses turn silvery as if drizzled with snow in a warm day and seasoned with the scent of mint. "Lucy!" he called out, hoping she'd bear witness.

"Okay, I'm done!" Lucy stood up.

Meanwhile, Harold untied his left shoe. "I tied you tight and now this!" he roared. Shaking off his shoe, his jaws dropped when he caught a ruby the size of a grape tomato. He looked on closely. It had a small imprint of a black snake which he thought moved for a split second. He shook his head, deeming that what he saw was just trick of the eye. He then looked around while secretly slipping the stone into his left pocket. He then wore his shoe casually. He started toward his siblings, whistling a merry tune, feeling lucky. Reaching Eli's spot, he saw him doubled over, scorched by the daylight filtering through the leaves. "What's wrong with you?"

Lucy stepped over. She almost dropped the flowers after seeing Eli's posture. "Why are you breaking in sweat?" she asked, beginning to panic.

Harold prompted her to check his temperature. "Feel his forehead. Dad said last night he might have a fever," he remembered.

Argos, seeing their dark shadows closing in, spun around Eli, creating a bright haze, like a halo, leaving them behind the circle.

The wind swirled about, carrying his scent.

"Why does it smell like Vicks?" Lucy snorted heavily.

Harold sniffed hard. "Eli must have smothered himself with Vicks! He's the sick one!"

Eli groaned while trying to keep an eye on Argos's blinding orbit. He tried to catch his form, but his ears kept on ringing. He could a whirring sound grinding around him—Argos's flapping wings. Still, Harold's voice cut through the ringing. He told Lucy to go home and get their mother. Seeing their shadows about to leave, Eli glanced askance their way. "Can't you see? He's here!"

They stopped and gave him puzzled gazes.

"How come they don't see you?" Eli asked Argos.

"He's still Eli–*fied!*" Harold claimed.

"Stop this madness now!" Lucy called out in her stentorian tone. She marched forward, roaring in frustration. When her right foot stepped within an inch from the shadow Argos cast, he flashed to the diverging alley, dragging Eli along.

Harold and Lucy ran after him.

"Why are you running, Eli?" he yelled tautly.

"Maybe he saw a butterfly!"

"Stop joking, Lucy! We both know there was no butterfly!" he rebuked, in between puffs of breath.

"I know! I'm just feeling butterflies in my stomach!" she admitted, placing her hands over her nervous tummy.

"It better be a *pot of gold!*" he declared, tapping his left pocket.

The alley ran for a stretch and opened into a spacious forest. They gasped in mixed fear and awe at the picturesque preserved trees. The smell of the grass lingered thick.

"This is a rabbit trail," he murmured, backpedaling.

"We're not supposed to be here," she replied, feeling restless. "Reverend Goodfellow told us not to wander off this way. We disobeyed him!"

"Eli!!!!!" Harold screamed, feeling guilty and nervous at the same time.

The trees trustled.

"Come back, Eli!" Lucy shouted, stomping her right foot.

Harold listened for his reply. When Lucy opened her lips, about to say something, he shushed her. Shortly, his eyes widened in shock.

"Why?" she asked nervously, unable to keep silent for a minute.

"I hear twigs snapping. The ground is collapsing," he described, his face crumpled. "It sounds so close like it's happening right here," he continued, pointing to his feet. He jumped back, afraid the ground would suck him in.

Lucy shook her head, baffled by his narration. "You're like Eli. You're both imagining things."

Harold fidgeted. "You don't see it. You just *hear* it!" he claimed, growing uneasy. Suddenly, his face paled. "Oh my God! Someone fell off a cliff!"

"Eli!!!!!" Lucy screamed.

Chapter 12: The Transfiguration

Dirt piled over Eli, muffling his scream for help. He pushed his right leg hard to put a stop to his plunge, but he continued to slide down to the bottom of what looked like an abyss swarming with gnarling white snakes, which were actually protruding dry twigs. Darkness cloaked him over. He gasped, suffocating. About to faint, he saw through his muddied eyeglasses a light gleaming from below. In a blink, it exploded in his face.

Dazzled, he covered his eyes. His sliding came to stop. Suddenly, he was being pulled up, way up in the sky in a snap. The daylight was too warm that his pores started leaking in buckets. He took his next breath. The minty air filled his depleted chest. The blowing wind intensified. He looked down and was shocked to see the mud track he left on the gully. "Why am I flying? I have no wings!" he shouted, beginning to feel airsick. About to freak out, glowing clouds surrounded him. Suddenly, a face sliced through a cloud. Startled, he lost balance and plummeted.

"I'm gonna die!"

The smell of the rich soil and mountain laurels burned his lungs again. He touched down and saw his running feet. "I'm chasing who?"

Argos glided past him.

His eyes widened. "Harold! Lucy! It's the mini-comet!" he shouted, feeling amazed at how Argos blazed the path without burning the bushes. "Wish we can record this!" When he heard no response, he made a full backward glance and found them missing. His face paled. "I'm an idiot! I left them behind!" he rambled, doing a face-palm. About to twist his foot to look for them, the wind carried Argos' voice to his ears.

"Eyes on the *prize*."

Eli's heart jumped. He panned back and was grazed by a protruding dry branch. "Ouch!" he cried, touching his left cheek. Blood oozed from the cut. He pressed on. Suddenly, his feet lost steam. A thought nagged him. "How can I go home when our house is back there?" he wondered, sticking his right thumb behind himself, which quickly went limped with fatigue. "Why did that thought cross my mind? He's the one going home!" he shouted, pointing to Argos's glowing trail.

The trees cheered. The branches danced like palm leaves welcoming his presence. He furrowed his eyebrows, weirded out. "Why is this place speaking back to me? This is my first time here, but it feels like I've been here before," he said, trying to shrug off the feeling of connection. He pondered about it for a moment. His face lit up. "My thoughts are pointing to a great revelation ahead!" he concluded, speeding up.

Argos shifted to first gear.

The hurried chase turned measured.

Eli let out an incredulous gasp when he finally saw a form inside Argos's radiance—strips of what looked like white cloth fluttering in a rhythmic wave. "Wow! Your suit is cool!" he shouted, curling his fingers. He tried to grab a piece, but the accompanying glow hurt his eyes. Worse, his migraine returned.

Argos, seeing his dirty hand about to touch his right wing, pulled his shoulders in and hovered up.

Eli came to a grinding stop. "Where did you get your gravity-defying shoes?" he wondered while trying to see his feet behind the flying dust.

In a twinkling of an eye, Argos transfigured. Bright rays beamed from his gilded armor. He descended slowly, his glowing huge white wings spread wide behind him.

"A-n angel?" Eli stood paralyzed.

Argos landed. The sky turned cloudy over him, muting his radiance.

Eli gasped. Heart-shaped face, dwarf ears, long, blond eyelashes raking in so beautifully, aquiline nose, piercing blue eyes sparkling like sapphires, brawny chest and arms, six feet tall, and fluffy, minty-scented, stork-like wings, he described Argos as a fantasy superhero hauled out straight from Lucy's books! He figured the wing stencil on his gilded breastplate spoke of his allegiance. He estimated his age should be in the early twenties. He looked past him and marveled quietly at his long, golden mane blown by the wind. The strands looked like layers of flowing silk. Something sparkled on the ground. He checked his feet and saw the crystal spikes on his boots. They looked like icicles under the heat of the day. The sharp tips glinted. He moved back, afraid to get poked.

"But angels always bring good tidings," Eli thought hopefully.

Argos's memory stone blinked wildly. He sniffed hard, smelling a whiff of blood. His eyes fluttered nervously, afraid his enemies would find the scent. He quickly made a self-scan. He had no wound. He turned to Eli. His left cheek showed a carmine streak. Alarmed, he flashed to his spot. He quickly raised his right hand in the air.

Eli tried to dodge his hand. "P-please don't hurt me," he begged. A bright, warm light slapped him, followed by a tightening on his left cheek.

Argos pulled his hand away, the healing light in the middle of his palm fading. "I just healed your wound," he said, retreating.

"W-why is your hand burning?" Eli stammered. He touched his left cheek and found his cut gone. "You stitched my cut and made it vanish! What is this magic?" he queried, deeply awed. His countenance change, sensing he posed no danger at all.

Argos bowed on his left knee. "My name is Argos," he introduced. "I am a *Lucere*, from the kingdom of Shadow Lights, armor-bearer of the true king," he continued, hoping in his heart their conversation would prove productive, given the short time.

"Argos. *Lucere*. Shadow Lights," he repeated. "You're not the albino?"

"No. I was the one who ruined your dinner last night. For that, I apologize," he admitted, smiling impishly. "I'm sorry I did that trick. I just had to test your gift of sight."

Eli froze. His magical stint flashed back. "D-dude! You broke into our house! That's gonna land you in jail!" he accused, trying to put up a strong front.

"Well, I just escaped from my prison yesterday." Argos's face grew long.

"And you want to go back right away!" Eli rolled his eyes.

Argos nodded sadly. "I have to. I need to free the remnants," he replied. "That's why, I need to find the book—the *Chronicles of Light*. That's why I was in your house." He pressed his face forward, hoping to get a clue from Eli's reaction.

Eli pulled his head. "First of all, our house is not a library! I was planning to go to the library today to get the book to explain *you*, but you're already here! You can do the explaining yourself! But here you are, telling me you need a book too!" he declared, at length.

Footsteps resounded.

Alarmed, Argos reached for his sword. Before he could pull it out, Harold and Lucy appeared, both dirt-caked and wheezing heavily. He snapped his sword back, then flashed away in a split second.

"Eli!!!!" both shouted.

"Lucy! Harold!" Eli embraced his siblings, deeply relieved.

Lucy went right away in her scolding. "It's your fault that we look like zombies! We were exhumed!" she blasted, pointing to her dirty dress. "And my flowers are gone! I managed to save just one!" she sobbed, showing him a wilted piece.

Eli petted the flower. "I'm sorry for this," he apologized, adding, "And yes, I missed you too. But how did you find me?"

"*Dumbo* played it by the ear," she revealed, sticking her right thumb toward Harold, who pulled his earlobes. "Yeah, he doesn't mind the tag now."

Harold grinned. "I don't know how. I just listened," he admitted. "Dad said I have chops too. The only downfall was our plunge. We're like *Jack and Jill* tumbling down that gully. Worse, we were soaped with moss!" He smelled his collar and frowned.

Argos covered his nose.

He continued, "That gully was high and steep. Good thing Lucy and I slid off easily. That would have been really painful."

Eli slipped into reflecting. He recalled the beam of light shooting up from the bottom. His eyes fluttered. "So, it was you," he whispered, glancing at Argos, who gave him a quiet shrug.

"But why do you have itchy—wandering—feet?" Lucy probed.

"If only your eyes and mouths could spank, I already took a beating," he frowned, disliking the heat. "But I didn't mean to stray away. I, um, I had to follow...*him*," he said, stretching his left hand toward Argos.

"A-an angel?" Lucy couldn't believe her eyes.

Harold snickered in contempt. "Is this some kind of a prank, Eli? You made us chase you all the way here so that you can meet up with this dude in angel's costume?" He then pushed him on the shoulder. "Dude," he said, turning to Argos, "You're way too early for the *Trick or Treat!*"

Eli pulled him aside. "Don't talk to him in that tone. He has powers and a sword. A real sword," he whispered, pointing his lips to his sheath. "His name is Argos. He is a *Lucere*. From the kingdom of Shadow Lights, he's the armor-bearer of the true king."

Harold laughed nervously. "*Lucere*? *Shadow Lights*? Why do you believe him?" he retorted, throwing off Argos. Noticing he made him uncomfortable, he continued, "He's the ring thief! He ditched his black hoodie and donned this costume to trick you!"

The clouds cleared out. Argos radiated once more. His gilded armor and the crystal spikes on his boots sparkled. The metallic plates on his armor and vambraces made long, straight light rays, while the wing stencil on his chest glimmered.

"Whoa!" The siblings covered their eyes, briefly dazzled. When their eyes adjusted to the glare, they moved forward to observe him.

"Is that a butterly?" Lucy pointed to his chest.

The sky turned cloudy again. Argos's radiance became more muted. "I-I'm sorry. I thought you were enemies," he apologized meekly.

Harold's jaws dropped. "Ey! I know your voice!" he nervously claimed.

"Y-you know you had an outburst last night, right after you went to bed," Eli told him, determined to tell the truth at last.

Argos shrugged and said, "I had to be sure he heard me the second time."

"W-what?" Harold stopped listening. "You were not in our room last night! That's impossible!"

"I was inside the walls," he admitted casually.

Eli recalled vividly. "You were the bright light that appeared from the mirror behind Lucy's seat! You sliced the air, over the table, and grabbed a bunch of grapes!"

"My favorite." Argos smacked his lips.

"Wait!" Harold shouted, stopping their dialogue. "I'm having trouble *digesting* his words."

Lucy chortled. "Digesting," she whispered, earning a dagger look from him.

"I can't *process* what he's saying," he reiterated, panning back to Argos immediately.

"Process," she repeated, smiling naughtily.

Harold tried hard to ignore her. "You said, the *second time*?" he pressed.

"I was simply reminding you that brothers shouldn't fight." Argos shrugged.

"R-right! That's how I remember it! But I thought I was hearing Dad in my dream," he recalled, looking perplexed.

"Dad was in your dream too?" Eli probed.

"Dad was *in* his room," Lucy cut in. "I slept in his room last night, remember?"

Harold placed his hand over her face, dismissing her. He then confronted Argos. "So, when was the first time?" he asked with crumpled face, partly awed to hear the truth and partly afraid.

"During the grace, when you stole Eli's final words," he revealed, irritating Eli. "I didn't know he has the gift of hearing," he explained. "That's why I tested him again. Just to be sure."

Harold grabbed his head. "Argh! H-how? You were not in our house last night!"

"He was!" Eli insisted.

"I didn't see him!"

Argos sneered. "Like I said, I was *hiding* inside the walls," he stressed out, silencing the brothers. Recalling how accommodating the space between the stone walls and the frames were, he calmed down and slipped into his pondering. "I see now. He saw my coming," he mumbled softly while rubbing his chin. He was surprised to discover he had grown a stubble, a proof of his distress as of late.

Harold paced back and forth, brooding. He stopped walking and started measuring Argos's size with his hands. His eyes squinted. "Stop *lying!* We're not stupid!" he grumbled, feeling insulted. "There is no way you'd fit inside the walls! For all I know, and this is what I believe—Eli told you everything you know before we came here, so he wouldn't be in a bad light again!" he accused, prompting Lucy to gasp.

Argos's nostrils flared. "I don't lie! Far be it! Check my shadow! That's my proof!" he snarled, displaying his protruding canines.

Eli and Harold looked down simultaneously.

"Whoa! What fancy boots you have!" Harold quipped, eyeing the crystal spikes.

"And what sharp teeth!" Lucy added, unable to stop gazing at his face. "Don't bite us, OK?"

"When we cross to the other side, check my shadow!" Argos started panicking. "We have to cross now! I can't afford another day!"

Eli checked his feet. "Shadow Lights," he mumbled softly, his eyes darting toward Argos's feet.

"Shadow? Heart?" Lucy looked confused.

"Our shadows show whether our hearts are pure or not," Argos curtly explained. "We need to find the book," he then told Eli. "Tell me where did Prince Elijah hide it?"

"Prince Elijah?" Eli's eyes drifted.

Argos's face lit up, sensing he had stirred up something. "Yes! Prince Elijah—your grandfather! Now, tell me!"

"Prince Elijah," Lucy and Harold chorused.

Eli fidgeted. "M-my dream. I-I thought that voice was calling for me. He was calling for Grandpa? But the mirror…" How he interchanged from an angel, to his Grandpa, then to himself flashed back clearly.

"Mirror?" Argos pressed his face close to his.

Eli pulled away. "You're way too close," he said, feeling discomfort. "As I was saying before you smothered me with this," he continued, gesturing with his hand over his face, "in my dream last night, there's this compact mirror that grew and turned into a door."

"A mirror into a door?" Argos looked puzzled.

"Well, it doesn't make sense, but that's what I saw. And inside that mirror was an herbal garden!"

Argos threw his clenched fist in the air. "I knew it!" he blurted out, startling the children. "I searched high and low and I didn't find the book! It's hidden somewhere in Shadow Lights! Argh!"

"I see you left something out," he mused. "But why do you call Grandpa Prince Elijah? Do you know him?"

Argos nodded. "He was my friend."

The children laughed.

"What's funny?" Argos furrowed his eyebrows.

"How old are you?" Harold snickered.

"Forty."

The children laughed harder.

Argos shrugged. "Well, it took some time for my mother to conceive."

"Your mother? How old is she?" Lucy asked.

"A century."

"How many is a century?"

"He's just playing us," Harold whispered, nudging her softly at her elbow.

Eli pondered his power of speed. "No, wait," he said. "Maybe the way they calculate time is different from us."

Argos shrugged. "That's what my Father said. You move slow, the sky is translucent…"

Eli continued, "You mean to say, you met Grandpa when he was younger? So, he is a…"

"A *Lucere*." Argos looked away; his eyes pinched with sadness.

Lucy tapped her chin. "Hmmm. So that's why Mom and Dad call me an angel all the time! I didn't know it was for real! I have the blood of an angel—or a *Lucere*. Looks the same to me!"

“Keep quiet, Lucy!” Harold rebuked. “Stop making this about you again! And don’t buy their story!”

Argos opened his lips slightly, muttering inaudible words.

Harold cupped his ears. “Stop it, Argos! You don’t need to scream at my ear!”

“You’re not serious.” Lucy snickered. “What did he say, if I may?”

“Believe and do not doubt,” Argos and Harold chorused.

“Oh my!” Lucy covered her mouth.

Eli nodded his head hard. “We are half-*Luceres*,” he told Harold, before turning his eyes on Argos, marveling at his appearance and powers. “Wow!”

“We call your kind *Gris*. You are *Grises*,” Argos pointed out, observing their tiny, dirty faces, before zeroing in on Eli. His eyeglasses threw him off, but he bounced back quickly. “You saw a glimpse of your grandfather’s memory, but how?” he wondered, glancing at his ring.

Eli shrugged.

Argos processed his dream. “An herbal garden?” he mused, looking confused. “I don’t think his nest had one. Plus, we have many herbal gardens in Shadow Lights. Which of them?” he sighed exasperatedly. “Did you find any of his personal possession at your house?” he asked Eli, suggestively.

“All we have are pictures,” he replied matter-of-factly, dampening his hopes. “Besides, Grandpa died when I was a toddler. All we know of him were hand-me-down stories told by our parents and Reverend Goodfellow, his best friend. Why I dreamt of him, I don’t know,” he replied in a breath of confusion.

"We really need to find that book. Our lives depend on it," he stressed out, hoping to drum up support.

"Why did Grandpa hide it?" Lucy asked.

"He took the book with him to keep it safe, from falling into the wrong hands," he explained, pulling in a deep breath after. "But our enemy is still looking for it so he could escape judgment and keep his reign of terror. I took comfort that the book was safe until now. You, Eli," he said, turning his face back to him, "it will listen to you."

"I have poor eyes. Why me?" Eli asked, as he looked down.

"Believe and do not doubt," Harold whispered to him.

"Are you encouraging me now?" he replied, surprised by his gesture.

Harold laughed. "Nope. I just like how the words roll off my tongue!"

"You saw me," Argos interrupted. "You have the gift of sight. You can find the book. It will listen to you."

"Y-yeah. I did," Eli replied, beginning to feel confident. He turned to Lucy and smiled. "Truth is out. He is the *talking mini-comet*," he said, feeling vindicated.

"True," she agreed, throwing Harold a stink-eye.

Argos shook his head. "No! The truth isn't out without the book! Find the book and reveal the past!" He flapped his wings hard.

The ground trembled.

Chapter 13: The Gray Border

The grasses peeled off and flew in heaps. Each heap rolled away in opposite directions. The children grabbed each other, terrified of being pulled up in the air. When the trembling subsided, they looked down and started gasping. The tarred ground looked like another gully in their eyes.

"Not again!" Harold flapped his arms.

Argos walked in. His wings were clipped.

The children's eyes widened.

"You're walking over the pit?" Lucy's jaws dropped and it stayed that way for a minute. She then stretched her both arms toward him. "Please, help," she requested.

"Stand up!" he ordered, smiling impishly.

The grasses pricked Eli's palms. "Ouch!" he cried, realizing promptly they were laying down over the dead ground. "Who did this? Who scorched the grasses?" he asked, jumping to his feet. He then pressed his toe hard against the dirt. "The ground is dead to its roots!" He straddled his arms out. "It goes in a straight line!"

Harold and Lucy stood up.

"Thank God!" Lucy pulled the flower to her chest and sniffed it avidly.

Harold snarled at Argos. "You killed the ground!"

Argos sneered. "You're so quick to point fingers. The ground isn't dead," he explained. "This is the Gray

Border, the line that separates your world from ours. We have lived side by side since time immemorial," he narrated, adding, "In your world, you wait for the sun to shine in the morning and for the moon to take its vigil throughout the night. In our world, the light never ends. We carry it with us." His brawny chest pumped forward, feeling proud.

The children exchanged confused looks.

Argos pointed to the east. "That is your world—Evergreen," he said. He then pointed to the west. "That is my world—Shadow Lights."

"How about the sun and moon you spoke about?" Eli inquired curiously.

"In your world, the light and darkness take turns. In my world, the light never ends."

"Even at night?" Lucy wondered. "That would be boring. The moon and the stars are beautiful at night."

Argos smiled. "Every night, rainbows appeared." His wings fluttered softly.

Harold glared at the ground. He stayed quiet, mulling. "What if we died in the plunge?" he asked his siblings, breaking his silence at last. "And what we are seeing now is our afterlife." His throat vibrated in fear.

"You mean, we… *resurrected?*" Lucy trembled.

"You didn't die! I caught you all!" Argos revealed.

Eli grabbed Harold's collar. "We didn't die!" he shouted.

Harold pushed him away. "Okay. Chill," he said, fixing his collar. "BTW, your breath stinks!" he added.

Eli smelled his breath.

"I'm just saying, everything is…surreal." Harold shrugged.

Eli noticed a spark in the bushes. He walked toward it and pushed his right hand through a gap. He gasped, feeling the rain dripping on his arm. He pulled it back quickly and was shocked to find it dry.

"We're not supposed to be here." Lucy materialized on his back.

Argos cut in. "Your grandfather's enemy will beat a path to your doorsteps! The only way to stop him from crossing to your world is by finding that book!"

"Grandpa never had enemies," she countered. "He was liked by everyone!"

Eli's eyes turned saucers. "The silhouette," he remembered.

"He does have an enemy. That's why he kept that book from him," Argos relayed.

"I get it now," Eli pondered softly, keeping the matter to himself. "Wait, Grandpa has the book, but the silhouette also has a book. Two books?"

Harold asked, "What if the book has been found?"

Eli's face turned pale. "No! It couldn't be! That book killed the light in the sky and the trees," he thought aloud, shivering in horror.

Argos shook his head. "The sun continues to shine in Shadow Lights. It means the book is safe somewhere for now. We need to find that garden," he stressed, highlighting each word.

Eli exhaled sharply. "That's a relief," he mused to himself.

"This isn't our fight! It was Grandpa's fight! He's been dead for years. Dead people don't fight anymore!" Harold stomped his feet.

"It is past to you, but it is present to us. Yet, we share the same future. Shadow Light's demise is Evergreen's too. The fight doesn't end with your grandfather's death. His enemy will find you," he guaranteed, clicking his tongue.

"What does he have against us?"

"You are Prince Elijah's seeds," he answered. "You have a great share in Shadow Lights."

"Y-you mean, we are rich?" Harold's eyes twinkled.

Lucy shushed him.

"That's the pot of gold I was talking about a while ago," he retorted softly.

"Never mind that, he'll fly us to the war," she whispered back. "We're only kids. We don't know how to defend ourselves."

"In my world, no one can lay a finger on you. Once the book is found, I will bring you home personally," Argos assured. His memory stone blinked, capturing his promise.

Harold grumbled at him. "Stop eavesdropping! We're having a private talk here! That's rude!"

Argos shrugged. "I can't help it. I hear every word you say. Even before you say it aloud," he replied. "Your mouths move slow."

Lucy noticed Eli was silent. "What are you thinking?" she asked, hoping he'd backpedal.

Eli took a moment to answer. "We need to find the right book," he said, earning puzzled look from Argos. "The *Chronicles of Light,* I believe, is a good read," he continued.

"Are you for real?" she fired back. "We're talking about a battle between *Luceres*. You said it yourself – they have powers and swords!"

"Then what are you scared of? He's on our side."

Lucy pondered. "Yeah. You're right," she agreed half-heartedly.

Harold pulled his earlobes. "We are *Grises!* We have powers too!"

"I have none." Tears quickly gathered in Lucy's eyes.

Eli touched her on the shoulder. "We have a share in Shadow Lights. We have relatives over there," he said, glancing back to the bushes. "Don't you want to meet them? Grandpa was a prince! You are a real princess, Lucy!" he said convincingly, feeling excited for her.

"You heard it, Harold," she replied, struggling to choke back her sentiments.

"Besides, I want to seek the truth. I want to know why Grandpa crossed the Gray Boder. That book has the answer."

"Oh, Eli," she mused, shaking her head. "In one night you changed big time. You want to tackle something bigger than you as if there's something big hidden inside your tiny body," she said, looking doubtful.

Eli lifted his hands close to his chest and made a quick spin. His eyes lit up, recalling how the ball of light he created killed the silhouette. "I can be a hero. I can save the day," he mumbled to himself.

Argos overheard. "Do save the day." Suddenly, his wingtips glowed bright, hit by a light faintly beaming out in a straight line from the bushes behind him. His heart jumped. "It's still day in Shadow Lights!" he shouted, only to halt his rejoicing after realizing that time did stop. "H-how? Was it the mirror in the dining room? No. Time ticked away," he remembered, turning to Eli. "But he saw the mirror only in his dream."

"I see. We're going on a field trip," Harold interrupted.

The light flickering through the bushes fainted.

"We must cross now while light remains," Argos prodded, looking wary.

"Argos," Eli called out."I will help you find your book, but you better make good on your promise. Bring us home safely. Don't make our parents worried sick."

"Time flies fast in Shadow Lights. It's just going to be a flyby." Argos swallowed hard, recalling how the day in Shadow Lights faded fast.

Eli grabbed Lucy's right hand. "Are you excited?" he asked, hoping to convince her.

Lucy shook her head. "What about our school?"

"We're still going to school."

"What do you mean?"

"Our school is that way," he said, pointing to the west. "I determined today that I'll find the book that will unmask him," he continued, tilting his head against Argos. "Seems like my mission remained the same."

"B-but, I don't know how to read."

"Have courage and be kind. Where there is kindness, there is goodness," he narrated, making her eyes flutter. "And where there is goodness, there is…"

"…magic!" she finished, with her tiny hands clasped over her chest. "Oh, I love Cinderella!"

Harold took a deep breath. "I'm now beginning to regret why we're not homeschooled, like that rich kid! Geez!" he exclaimed. "They better have plenty of food or I'm out!"

"When we cross the Gray Border, keep your heads up. It's really a short walk. Trust me," Argos instructed, hiding the anxiety in his face. He turned around and exhaled sharply before making his way to the bushes. Before their eyes, he vanished.

"W-where did he go?" Lucy panicked.

"I'm here," he replied, his voice slightly muffled.

Eli drew in. He pushed his right hand against the bushes. Part of his arm vanished. "Look," he told his siblings, to their wonder. From the wall, Argos pulled him in hard. Eli dragged Harold, who pulled Lucy along. A bright light sucked them in.

The peeled grasses rolled back.

Chapter 14:
The Witness Stones Will Tell

The streaming wall of lights dazzled the children. The moment they crossed, a dark sky and heavy storms greeted them.

"Take shelter," Argos instructed, his wings spread to cover his head like a canopy.

They ran for cover.

"The sky is so mad," Lucy observed, shivering.

"Where did the light go? Why is there a storm?" Eli asked, his mouth gagged by the pouring rain.

Argos carried them up—Harold in his left arm, and Lucy and Eli swaddled in his right arm. He whirled about. Below him, the chasm howled. The children screamed. The raging dark waters tried to lick their feet. They lifted their feet up to their bellies and grasped Argos's arms tightly, but the pouring water made their grip slip.

"Just look up!" Argos ordered. He hovered over the chasm, but the strong wind and rain tried to push him down. He fought back.

Harold heard loud growlings from inside the pit. He closed his eyes firmly and cupped his ears.

Ahead, a beacon flickered in the midst of the blur. Eli focused on it, thinking it was a lighthouse. Soon, it multiplied and exploded in his face.

Argos travailed. Reaching the edge, the wall of streaming light pulled them in.

Eli landed after him. The dry grasses crunched under his feet. He crouched, dazzled by the bright sky. A gentle breeze blew his way. He took a deep breath and felt refreshed. "Huh! The storm stopped!" he blurted out, deeply shocked.

Greenish light sparkled in the air. He wheeled around and saw what looked like sparkling emerald stones floating in midair. His misty eyes calibrated. The towering, luscious white oaks gently swayed. Its leaves looked like emerald stones under the glittery sky. "Glitters?" His eyes zoomed to the sky. He gasped in awe. It looked like a suspended ocean with sparkly ocean waves. He feasted on it, wondering how he could see everything as airborne. While marveling, the colorful neon glitters evaporated. The wind blew in. His face crumpled, smelling something awful.

Harold and Lucy yelped from behind. He cranked his neck and saw them paddling their arms, swimming in light, on their feet. He quickly grabbed their hands and pulled them out. The glittery sky took him back.

"I'm wet! I need a new dress!" Lucy cried. She touched her head. "Wait, why is my hair dry?" she wondered, pulling out a flaky strand. "Euw!" she grimaced.

The ticking hands on her analogue watch spun fast, unbeknownst to her.

"There's water in my ears!" Harold tapped his head repeatedly. His ears rang. The blowing wind added its frequency to the ringing in his ears. It sounded like a squall. He thought he was still inside the Gray Border. But when he realized the serenity at hand, he calmed down. Lucy approached him. The brittle grasses under her soles crackled like fireworks. He grimaced. "The sounds are amplified."

"We're out of the storm." Her voice echoed in his ears.

"H-how come?" He glanced back and saw the wall of streaming lights. He steered away from it. "I don't want to go back in there. There are beasts inside that chasm," he said, trembling.

"Did you see any?" Her voice started to sound normal in his ears again.

Harold shook his head.

Lucy smiled. "We're past the storm," she comforted. "We're on the bright side now," she added, pointing to the sky.

The towering canopies swayed.

"Those trees are the height of a building." Lucy deflated.

"Jack planted these giant brocollis," Harold replied, awed.

"Who's Jack?"

"You don't know Jack? The guy in *Titanic*," he replied, recalling the storm.

"Hmm. I don't know him."

Harold smirked. "I meant, *Jack and the Beanstalk*, silly bugger! You're so slow!"

"I know that story! Obviously, you like it because of the treasure," she said, rolling her eyes. "Jack is a thief. First he stole a gold coin, then a chicken laying golden eggs. And, as if that weren't enough, he climbed up the beanstalk to steal a magical harp! Greedy!"

"Duh! I didn't ask you to tell me the entire story! Besides, he did that for his mother!" he argued. "The means justified the end!"

"Nu-uh!" Lucy gave him a stink-eye.

Harold noticed Eli continued to eye the sky. He pointed his lips toward him. "Look at him," he told her. "Eli-*fied*..."

"The sky is filled with glitters," Eli declared, who had been listening all along.

"How can we see the sky when the canopies are blocking it?" Harold tried to see past the blinding sky.

Eli frowned. "Huh? But I can see it clearly from here," he said, sliding his fingers inside his eyeglasses after. "Must be my gift of sight."

"Because you're farsighted," she identified.

Eli snorted. His face soured. "The sky looks so sweet, but it smells bad."

"Sweet but bad?"

"That doesn't sound right," Harold said, pushing his right index against his ear.

Dead leaves fluttered their way.

"Whoa! Why is it fall suddenly?" Eli was puzzled.

"Nu-uh! Don't tell me it's winter tomorrow. We're not dressed up for that!" Lucy grabbed the hem of her dress.

"Weird," Harold mused, catching the mildewed parts of the leaves.

From the corner of his eye, Eli noticed a spark of light. He turned around and saw the dirty tunnel. "Whoa! Look over there!" he declared, prompting his siblings.

Lucy clasped her hands, feeling excited. "Like a castle!"

Eli's eyes focused on the sparkly lights running in a straight along the wall. "Crystal stones," he figured.

Argos shushed them.

"Oh there he is!" Lucy said, finding him a block away. "But why is he grumpy?"

"He has issues," Eli replied.

Harold sneered. "Yeah! He wants to read a book!"

Argos shushed them again.

Harold stepped forward to probe. He turned the side of his face and listened. His ears took him inside the gate, past the tunnel. He heard movements in the trees. He moved back. "I don't want to go in there," he declared, feeling iffy.

"That's the only entrance I see," Lucy objected.

"I heard something."

"You hear a lot!"

Argos snorted heavily.

Harold turned his face his way. "Argos is smelling the bushes and the trees," he relayed.

Eli looked up. "He smelled it too?"

Argos exhaled sharply, upset over Harold's eavesdropping. He took another deep breath in and said, "There's no alcohol residue. The drunkard cupbearer didn't hold vigil." He released his right hand off his sheath, then headed to the children. He glanced briefly at the streaming wall of light behind them, then gave them a curious look. "Are you all okay?" he asked, folding his dry wings.

"You mean the *storm?*" Eli retorted, shaking his head. "You didn't mention anything about it so you can string us along."

Argos sighed, his hands on his waist. "Crossing from your world to my world can't be a walk in the park," he argued. When none of them could find a word to rebut him, he grinned, enjoying the silence.

"It was scary, you know," Eli said at last.

"True."

"You said it was just a short walk. It wasn't!" Harold contended. "And that chasm, well, I heard loud growlings. What if we lost our grip and fell? Those beasts could have eaten us up!" He shivered at the possibility.

"You crossed safely."

Eli exhaled. "You better make good of your promise bringing us home. That's an impossible crossing to make."

"Pinkie-promise?" Lucy asked, sticking out her right little finger.

Argos nodded. "Come now. But please try to lessen the volume and speak less, so we don't wake up those sleeping," he requested, giving Harold a side glance.

"That was for solely me," he said, feeling insulted.

Lucy asked, "Why do your people sleep way too early?"

Argos struggled to explain. About to open his lips, Eli suddenly jumped in. "What did you smell?" he asked.

"Nothing."

Lucy wedged herself in between them. "What are those stones on the wall?" she asked, pointing to the tunnel.

"Those are witness stones." His face turned wary.

"What are *witness stones*?" Harold's interest was piqued.

"They're like, um, binoculars," he explained, dampening his enthusiasm.

Eli checked the stones. "What for?"

"To see those coming in. They also record those who crossed last."

"Like a video camera? Wow!" Lucy covered her mouth. "Ooopsie."

"Hey! We're here!" Eli jumped up and down, waiving his hands.

Harold stopped him.

Argos panicked. He spread his wings wide to block their view. "No one is watching."

Lucy leaned toward Eli and whispered, "They're still sleeping."

"He's right. No one's there," Harold agreed, feeling nervous.

Argos gave him a curious look. "What have you eaten?"

"Cereal and milk," he replied. "And I'm beginning to worry what will happen to our dinner if your people don't wake up."

Eli and Lucy rolled their familiar eyes.

"Where to?" Harold asked.

"To the *City of Refuge*. That's where I live," Argos replied. "But we're not going in through the *Omniscient Gate*."

"*Omniscient Gate*," Eli repeated. "Cool name."

"Why not?" Lucy tailed holding a puzzled look.

"Duh! You're not listening," Harold rebuked.

Argos pumped his right arm twice. "Hurry! I've learned a shortcut." He led them to the northeast, past the unmanned, gateless entrance, staying away from the reach of the witness stones. A secluded, narrow pathway covered with thick shrubbery appeared. He groaned. A plucked feather flew across his face. Annoyed, he quickly clipped his wings tightly. "I hate this," he mumbled to himself, grabbing the feather and inserting it back in.

"I like shortcuts," Eli smiled.

Harold sneered. "Yeah. Your shortcut to school led us here."

"Eli lied. There was no shortcut," Lucy protested. "My feet are tired."

"Well, you're wearing flat shoes. Obviously, walking is hard on your feet," Eli said.

"Even in winter, she wears dresses and flat shoes." Harold laughed.

Lucy raised her right fist, about to strike. "Will you stop checking my outfit!"

"Cool it," Eli meddled.

Lucy grumbled at Harold before speeding up. She stubbed her right foot on a protruding root. She stumbled, earning a sarcastic laugh from him. "Whatever!" she retorted while leaning on the wall to steady her balance. The grime on the wall pricked her palm. "Euw!" she cried, pulling her hand away. "If only there was a rain shower in this part too. These walls need a bath," she complained.

Argos kept on checking up on them. "Slow bills," he said, growing impatient.

Eli heaved a disappointed sigh.

"What's wrong?" he asked, discarding his contempt.

Eli let Harold and Lucy walk ahead. "I just thought of Grandpa," he explained. "This is supposed to be a home-coming for him, with us here," he said, trying to drain the hurt from his tone. "I really want to meet our family here."

Argos turned his face away. "Not a good idea," he said.

"Gosh. I'm a *Gris!*" Eli skipped in joy. He glanced at his clipped wings and said, "It would be nice to have wings for sure."

Argos glanced to the sky. His eyes turned whimsical.

A light shone on Eli's tail, prompting him to slow down. He made a U-turn. As he approached the gate, he noticed a crystal stone, embedded in the tarnished wall, that was sparkling. He touched it. The stone popped out, like an eye glaring at him. Startled, he stepped back. From behind, he sensed company. He jumped around and saw his reflection, then another one on another stone. "Hah! It's like I have a twin!" he laughed nervously.

His voice echoed. More stones popped out. His image multiplied, filling the entire tunnel. The stones beamed like flashlights. He hunkered down, dazzled. Shortly, the lights faded. He straightened up and was shocked to see the stones closing their eyes and sinking back. He walked backward, hitting Argos on his way out.

"Please don't do that again. You'll kill me!" he cried out, clutching his chest.

"Same here! Out of the tunnel right now!" Argos fumed.

Eli sheepishly stepped out, head bowed down. "I'm sorry."

"It is a *must* that you stay close to me. You are the *head* not the tail. Do bear this in mind." He headed back and came to a halt after a few steps. He glanced back, looking wary. "Now they will know you're here." His words trailed off.

The clamped pathway reached a turnoff. Harold and Lucy stood up, seeing them approaching.

"Here comes the *itchy feet*," she scowled.

"You didn't even say sorry for leaving us behind a while ago!" Harold confronted.

Eli fixed his eyeglasses to hide from their accusing glares. "Seriously? You're both keeping tabs? Dad spoke about *love* last night," he argued flatly.

Harold sneered. "So, you expect us to give you a *free pass* after everything? How about show some accountability?"

"Well, aren't you happy you reached this spot first? You won again."

"Oh yeah!" he realized.

Argos shushed him. "Refrain from talking too much or you will be heard."

Harold's nostrils flared. "Why are you on me? He's the one who strayed behind!" he blasted, earning another shush.

Lucy leaned against him. "Because your voice is too loud. That's why you always get booted out of the library," she pointed out softly.

"It's my natural voice. What can I do?" Harold spoke in his tiniest voice.

"Try using your bedroom voice," she suggested, clamping her right index and thumb over her mouth.

Harold cleared his throat. "B-but this is my bedroom voice."

Argos shook his head. "Still loud."

"Then try using your washroom voice," she goaded, bringing Eli to a chuckle, which he quickly restrained after Harold gave him a black look.

"One day, you'll all miss my voice," he told them off.

Argos stuck his right thumb up. "You are the *voice* of your siblings, but you must learn to speak in a timely way."

"You just shushed me a while ago and now you say I am the *voice?* What an irony!" he cried out. "I received a strong rebuke, while Eli here got a slap on the wrist for dawdling."

"He rebuked me too, for straying back there," Eli admitted, his cheeks red.

Harold started to calm down, appeased by his admission. "At least he gave me a new title for today. I am the *voice*," he said, lifting his collars up.

"And I am the…"

A scrubbing noise erupted.

Argos clawed a mortar. Dust trickled. The children coughed. He panicked, not wanting to catch the enemies' attention. He kept looking toward the south where the Omniscient Gate was, then at the trees. He dug faster. His fingers turned white and inflamed. A cloud gathered. The children coughed harder. He touched something. He stopped scrubbing. He quickly leaned forward and whispered inaudible words against it. The bottom of the wall shook, creating a door. The coughing ceased.

"Finally," Lucy sighed in relief; her nose pink in color.

"What was that about?" Harold dusted off his shirt.

"The shortcut," Eli mused.

Argos pushed the door. A hazy garden greeted them.

Chapter 15:
To the City of Refuge

"Get in!" Argos commanded.

Eli went in first. He glided his fingers against the wall. "This wall is packed with muscles!" No wonder there's too much dust! This is like what…three meters wide?" he calculated, his voice bouncing. "It's like I'm walking in a tunnel." He suddenly remembered the witness stones. He quickly pulled his hands away, as if electrocuted, and trod in the middle, walking in a straight line, away from the walls.

"We take pride in our discretion. Nothing comes in and out, unless warranted," Argos explained while prompting for Lucy and Harold to follow.

Lucy made her stride longer. "I wonder what else he can do, aside from creating a door from a wall," she whispered to herself.

Harold snarled. "Well, from the looks of it, he can create a door in your room so he can pay you a visit any time he likes to."

"For sure!"

"But I need to tell Mom and Dad about it before he can even knock!"

"He can sink in the walls and hide, right?" she recalled, adding, "So he doesn't need a door."

"Tsk. You're too young to be giddy over a man, rather, over a *Lucere*."

Argos overheard.

Eli stepped out of the wall. He stood at attention, connecting his dream to the garden at hand. Thorns, thistles and briers ran aplenty. "This isn't what I saw in my dream."

A fuzzy scent lingered.

Lucy and Harold covered their noses.

The grinding noise returned.

They all turned around. The wall closed before Argos.

"That wall is voice activated," Eli said, feeling amazed.

Harold's eyes blinked wistful.

Lucy noticed. "Spill it!"

"Well, I just thought," he began, stroking his tummy, "it would be nice if everything is voice activated. I want food. Poop!"

"Your thoughts and words are laced with food."

"*Laced*," Harold laughed. "Sounds so girly. So *princessy*."

Eli laughed, earning a push from Lucy.

"FYI, besides food, I found another fancy," Harold revealed, only to regret opening up. "Well, let's be honest. Eli wants to read a book. You have a crush. While I…" He paused, seeing Argos walking by. His eyes landed on the crystal studs on his boots.

"Come along now," he prodded, looking relaxed.

Eli trailed after.

"So, what's your new fancy?" she pressed.

Harold shrugged.

"Grr! You held me up!" Lucy gave a chase.

A giant dandelion blocked them. Along the banks, humongous weeds the size of a person's head stood erect.

Argos panicked quietly. He checked the sky. The sulfuric blaze filtered through but was muted.

Eli recalled the flowers in his dream.

"Like yellow umbrellas! I want one, Eli!" Lucy clapped her hands.

"Those dandelions will eat that flower in your hand," he replied, glancing at her wilted forget-me-not.

Lucy hid her flower. "Don't they have gardeners?" she fretted. "Mom skims these weeds off our backyard, pulls out its roots and *burns* them all."

Argos remembered the dead memory stones. His eyes mellowed.

Something whipped the air.

Alarmed, he grabbed the hilt of his sword and spun around, only to freeze after seeing Harold whacking a weed off his path with a stick.

"Wow! You hit it well," Eli praised.

"I don't like its smell."

Eli looked up. "Same."

"The smell is a diversionary tactic. It will keep our scents off the radar," Argos explained matter-of-factly.

"Our scents?" Eli wondered.

Argos glanced briefly at the patches of mosses and mudstains in their dirty clothes. "I mean, my scent, not yours," he clarified.

"From who?" Eli became suspicious.

Argos fidgeted, at a loss how to explain.

A feathery light hovered over his head, capturing everyone's attention. It swirled over his face, tickling his nostrils. He swatted it away like a fly, but it bounced on Lucy's head before drifting off to a diverging trail.

Lucy chased it. "Your heart! Your heart!" she repeated in glee.

"Don't wander off," he warned, to no avail. He flashed away to follow her, leaving Eli and Harold in the dust.

Harold's jaws dropped. "Where did he get those boots?" he asked enviously.

Eli prompted him to follow quickly.

Argos found Lucy standing still in front of a tree covered with a thick mist. Red balls twinkled brightly behind the mist like Christmas lights. His eyes widened. The feathery light joined the mist. A red ball sucked it.

Lucy gasped in shock. "It ate your heart!"

Argos flapped his wings. The mist moved away, revealing a dead tree with red, shiny apples.

Eli appeared. "How can a dead tree bear such fresh fruits?" he probed, feeling shocked and awed at the same time. He checked the roots. "Decayed!"

Harold showed up. The red color spoke to him. "Oh-la-la! I want one!" He ran toward it to grab a piece, but Argos stopped him with his flapped wing. "You don't want to eat the *Fruits of Darkness!* Those apples are poisonous!"

"The *Sleeping Death*," Lucy gasped in horror.

Harold blinked hard, as if awakened from a deep sleep.

"No wonder your people are asleep. They eat those apples," Eli told Argos.

Argos shook his head hard. "We don't eat those! Far be it!" he replied, feeling insulted. "One bite and your mind will be darkened!"

Harold trembled. "Let *Snow White* take a bite!" he said, pointing at Lucy. "Put her to sleep so she stops wandering off!"

Eli shushed Harold. "Don't give her the idea," he said, glancing at Argos. "No *true love kiss* for you," he then told Lucy. "Now who has the itchy feet?"

"You're contagious," she replied, blushing.

Argos noticed fresh scrapes on the trunk. "The *Deorcs* are now awake!" Alarmed, he pulled out his sword and spread his wings wide, shielding the children. He scoured the treetops.

"*Deorcs?*" Eli asked. "You said no one can hurt us here."

Flapping wings boomed in the sky.

"Nasty crows?" Harold asked, recalling his encounter.

Argos panicked. "How many?"

Lucy dredged her memory. "Um. Five," she answered, sticking her palm out. Seeing her dirty fingers, she pulled her hand back.

The flapping of wings turned boisterous.

Argos led the children back to the trail. "No matter what happens, stay really close," he warned, pushing them into a dreadful silence.

Harold dropped his stick and pulled out his sling shot. "I'm not scared of crows!"

"What are you doing?" Lucy disapproved.

"We need to defend ourselves. This," waiving his sling shot, "is my weapon. Amazingly, I didn't know I have the gift of hurling stone until today."

"But…"

"Shoot first, ask questions later."

Lucy turned to Eli, but he already picked up the stick Harold dropped. "This isn't another sword game of yours!"

"Keep quiet. We're not going at each other," he replied, swatting the air with the stick.

Argos came to a screeching stop. The flapping wings closed in, a flock of five, just like Lucy had said. He clenched his sword. The blade started blazing. The wings landed. Volume of footsteps boomed. He quickly looked for a place to hide the children and found a huge tree hollow. He hid them. "Stay here," he said.

"Your sword is on fire," Eli said, awed.

Argos shushed him.

Nostrils flared.

"They found my scent!" He quickly covered the mouth of the tree hollow with a rolled bale of hay.

The bushes behind him moved. Frantic footsteps closed in. He exhaled deeply. His sword blazed wildly. He pivoted and lunged when an explosion of colorful, bright lights jumped on him.

The hay turned colorful.

"A rainbow?" Eli mused.

Argos punched his sword back.

Curious, Eli crawled out. He followed the rainbow cast on the ground. His eyes grew as large as saucers. Five colorful football-sized lights—blue, purple, yellow, green and orange—swirled around Argos.

"Your candle of life remained aglow!" said the bluish ball of light in a woman's voice.

"Your mother is relieved!" The purple light's voice sounded sweet.

Argos choked back his tears. "But why did you step out? You left the city unmanned," he said, beginning to worry.

"The *Council of the Wings* sent us to find you," the bluish light replied.

The green ball of light whizzed toward Argos's face. "Wow! Look at his eyes!" it said in a cheery man's voice.

Oohs and aahs erupted.

Harold overheard. "We have company," he told Lucy.

The *Luceres* overhead him.

Eli hid behind the tree as they turned frenzied. They rallied behind Argos. His face was red, to his bewilderment.

The orange light pushed him on the shoulder. "What have you done? You were supposed to get the *book.* Just the book," the alpha voice behind the glow growled.

Argos meekly looked over his shoulder. "The *Chronicles of Light* never crossed the Gray Border."

"It can't be." The green light fell from its orbit.

"So, where is *he?*" The yellow light blinked brightly, feeling excited.

"He's dead," he relayed, earning bitter groans from everyone. "That's why I brought in his *seeds*. They will find the book."

"Seeds? You mean, *Grises*? More than one? At his age? Impossible!" The orange light said, at length.

Argos saw Eli's silhouette from behind the tree. "Come out, Eli," he prodded.

The *Luceres* repeated his name, all shocked.

Eli firmly stepped forward, holding his stick. His eyes glowed radiantly before them.

The lights fell from their orbits.

"A *Gris!*" the purplish light bellowed.

"He wears eyeglasses!" the green light hollered.

"Oh, you are mistaken, Argos!" the yellow light accused.

The orange light chuckled sarcastically.

Eli covered his eyes. "Can you please soften your glows?" he requested, adding, "It's my migraine."

"He can see us?" The purple light flickered.

Argos nodded. "He has the gift of sight."

"Why didn't you heal the poor boy?" the blue light grumbled.

"I did." Argos was confused.

Harold jumped out of his hiding with his sling shot. "Who's there? Show yourselves!" he shouted bravely, only to calm down after finding Eli and Argos by themselves. "Was it you speaking in a woman's voice?" he asked Argos.

A shadow fell on them.

"*Umbra*," the blue light mumbled in horror.

"Who said that? What's *Umbra?*" Harold aimed his sling shot against the dimming bushes.

The sulfuric blaze twinkling behind the towering trees was muted. Dark clouds started rushing in from the horizon. Around them, the woods turned gloomy.

"Lucy," Eli called out. "Here comes your rain."

"I hear listless breathing," Harold interrupted.

Lucy appeared. "It's cold," she said, shivering. She looked up. Thick clouds emerged. "Those clouds are not friendly!"

"We have to run! Come, follow me!" Argos prompted.

Something bright sparkled on the ground, like a spilled water.

Lucy saw his shimmering shadow forming. "Your shadow lights up!" Her eyes twinkled. "I get it! Shadow Lights!"

Darkness multiplied.

A turbulence of flapping wings erupted from the east.

Harold halted. "Crows!" He checked Argos's wings, comparing its size to the noise. "Your people are awake!"

Argos shook his head. "They're not my people!" His ears stood stiffly. He could hear them snorting heavily. He looked to his friends. Their plucked feathers flew everywhere. His pulse quickened. "Hurry!" he shouted.

"Where to?" Lucy complained, at a loss which path to take.

"Just follow the lights!" Eli admonished.

"What lights are you talking about? I can't see any! Do you have night vision?" she fired back, almost stumbling.

"Follow me!" Eli stayed focus on the *Luceres.* They blazed the woods, like grounded comets. Their memory stones made rainbow rings. The wind howled. It sounded like a beast daring for a fight. Their lights blinked wildly as they scurried away, like the scattered fireflies. He looked up to check on the moon, but he couldn't find it. The glittery sky bled out. "Argh! I spoke too soon! This is the night in my dream, which I said is about to happen a while ago!" he remembered, feeling conflicted as to how his dream and his reality at hand were linked. "Am I sleepwalking?" He wanted to ask Harold to pinch him, but he was running at the farthest end, so he pinched himself hard, on the right cheek. It did hurt. "I'm not dreaming!" he realized. As he followed the *Luceres,* he relieved his dream. "The silhouette ran scared because of my light," he mulled, sensing something strong stirring up within him. "Stop! We can stop this darkness!" he shouted, but a thick mist blocked him, isolating him from the rest, and muting his voice. He waddled, drowning in the sea of darkness he likened to the pile of dirt folding over him in the gully. He shivered. The cold breathed on his neck, up to his ears, like a frozen lips with a forked tongue, whispering words.

"Out of the ground comes a sound that will bring light into plight!"

His face turned pale. *It's the spell the silhouette chanted from the book!* He wanted to shout it out, but he couldn't move. Something bit his right arm.

Argos flashed to his side. He flapped his wings hard, dispersing the thick mist. He noticed the veins on his right arm were popping out, the skin turning papery. "A *Deorc* gave you this!"

"D-what?" Eli grimaced.

Argos carefully blew at his arm. White dust sparkled in the dark. It touched the stick in his hand and it charred away. The rest of the dust landed on the foot of a tree, turning its roots into a cement.

"H-how?" Eli stammered.

The squadron's glow exploded a block away.

"Let's go!" Argos carried Eli by his collar. "I'm sorry! But we need to hurry!"

Eli whimpered, feeling manhandled.

They reached a hillside.

"There's no castle here!" Eli cried out after landing. "This is a dead-end!"

Lucy almost stumbled on her way in. "My shoes gave up," she cried, showing her snapped heels.

Harold arrived last. "Where to?" he asked, breathing heavily.

The wind blew wintery. Flurries mixed. Everyone's hair turned gray, congealed by the blustering, icy wind drenching them through. Dark clouds came in escalating, thick waves, like torrents of a flood about to drown them in one spot.

"It's coming." Argos's face turned deathly pale.

In a blink, the squadron transformed: three men and two women, all dressed in gilded, knightly armor. Their chests bore wing stencils, similar to Argos's. They glowed according to their memory stones: amethyst, azurite, turquoise, garnet, and carnelian.

Harold and Lucy covered their eyes, thinking that a lightning had struck too close.

"Brace yourselves for a *melee*," the *Lucere* with the alpha male voice declared. He glowed sulfuric; his memory stone, a carnelian. He aimed his gilded longbow, which had golden sharp arrows, against the marching, clustered dark clouds. Its upper and lower limbs bore engraved wings.

Eli read the name etched on the arrow shelf. "Archer," he spoke softly, earning a side-eye from Archer. He skulked away, feeling threatened.

Harold heard Archer's voice. He opened his eyes and was shocked to see *Luceres* in battle formation.

"Copy that," said the *Lucere* beaming with bright-green light. His long, blond hair was tied in cornrows, revealing his turquoise-pierced petal ears—his memory stone. He spun a pair of white *tonfas*, a straight, wooden rod with a perpendicular handle attached. Its front and back ends looked like wings. Its shaft contained a blade. The name *Linus* was drawn on it.

The glowing, yellowish male, his memory stone a garnet, grunted while swinging his weapon—a huge, golden axe. Its crescent blade bore his name, *Lux*.

A voluptuous female carrying a thick, golden lance with *Roxanne* inscribed on its blade, which measured about five meters in length with a sharp, jagged tip, lunged forward aggressively. Her amethyst memory stone blinked wildly; its color camouflaged by the color of the night. She stood side-by-side with her female companion. Her heart-shaped face could be seen as she paced back and forth against the darkened bushes. Her azurite memory stone created multiple hazes, complementing her glowing, fierce blue eyes. The blue feather-and-lace headpiece with bluebells swayed in rhythm with the heavy, golden, spiky meteor hammer she carried handily. Each ball carried her name—*Pearl*.

The ground crackled, turning icy. Thick flurries gathered.

"It's winter," Lucy said, her tongue stuck to the roof of her mouth.

Harold trembled, hearing the blustering noise of flapping wings. "Those unfriendlies are coming in hot," he said, alarming the *Luceres*.

Argos pulled the children toward the hillside. He pressed his face against a stone and whispered, "Ephphatha."

The frosted vines crawled away, like retreating snakes. A grinding sound erupted. The stone rolled away.

"A cave?" The children exchanged confused looks.

"Get in!" Argos commanded.

Eli ushered his siblings in.

On her way in, Lucy took a quick glance and saw dark clouds approaching fast. She imagined it growling at her with angry eyes and big horns. Horrified, she stumbled, losing her grip on her wilted flower as a consequence.

"Lucy!" Eli shouted in panic.

Argos flashed to her side and carried her in. He checked the ground after. "Archer!" he called out, pointing to their footprints.

Archer hovered a few inches up the ground. The rest followed. In unison, they clapped their wings like cymbals, producing a strong airwave. Their footprints vanished, while the wilted flower rolled some distance away.

"NOW!" Argos summoned.

About to enter the cave, the shadow of night descended on the squadron. As if it bore limbs, it wrung their necks. Their faces turned blue instantly. Their glows fainted. They tried to swing their weapons but were impaled.

"No!!!!" Argos screamed, assailed with horror.

Archer gave him a stern look. "Close the door," he mouthed.

Argos clenched his jaws, determined to defy his order. He turned to the children and said, "You were really brave! I commend you! Now go to the City of Refuge!"

"B-but we can't see our way," Eli objected.

"Go find the *Lamp!*" he commanded, marshaling his wings. About to step out, he looked up to the ceiling briefly, then gave Eli a meaningful look.

Eli turned to his siblings. "We need to pray," he said, prompting them to sit down.

Lucy quickly clasped her hands and knelt. "Dear Lord Jesus, help us!"

Harold struggled to kneel down; his tight pants choked his legs. The ruby slipped out of his pocket, but he caught it in time. About to slide it back in his pocket, the shadow of night touched it. The snake imprint wiggled.

Argos brandished his sword. Its flame flickered against the cold. About to join the fray, the howling wind stopped. The flurries dwindled. The *Luceres* quickly transformed into balls of light. The moment the last ball – the orange light – entered the cave, the stone rolled over with the vines quickly spreading over it, hiding its mouth.

The dark sky collapsed.

The owl hooted.

Book Two: Shadow Lights and the Fruits of Light